Houses Borders Ghosts

Houses Borders Ghosts

The Fiction Desk Anthology Series
Volume Fourteen

Edited by Rob Redman

The Fiction Desk

First published in 2021 by The Fiction Desk Ltd.

ISBN 978-0-9927547-1-6

Please see our website for current contact details and submissions information.

www.thefictiondesk.com

Printed and bound in the UK by Imprint Digital.

Contents

Introduction

Rob Redman

Having produced an anthology on the theme of finding one's path, building momentum, and moving forwards (Volume 13, *Somewhere This Way*), it was perhaps inevitable that our series would promptly be overcome by global events and forced into a lengthy hiatus. Our contributors would not be daunted, however, and the period since our last anthology saw us receiving some of our richest and most interesting stories to date.

This volume features several recurring themes, sometimes combining within a single story: our relationship with the places where we live (a subject which has been at the forefront of many minds over the last year), is addressed in stories like Jacki Donnellan's 'Where the Breadcrumbs Go', Kate van der Borgh's 'Home, Time' and Clarissa Dennison's 'Pots'. Psychological borders and liminal spaces crop up several times, particularly in Zeph Auerbach's 'Desynchronisation at Seven Sisters', and as our regular readers will have come to expect, there's a supernatural tale or two to be found here as well.

Jacki and Kate have both appeared in our pages before, and Alastair Chisholm is also making a welcome return in this volume. The other authors are all new to us. There are so many talented writers out there; short stories, with the opportunities they provide for developing and showcasing skills, as well as experimenting with different styles and ideas, are the perfect way to discover them.

Jacki Donnellan introduces our housing theme with this story of a mysterious gift. 'Where the Breadcrumbs Go' is her second Fiction Desk work, following 'I Don't Blink' in Long Grey Beard and Glittering Eye.

Where the Breadcrumbs Go

Jacki Donnellan

'Do birds like breakfast cereal?' I ask my big sister.

She doesn't look up, but carries on staring at her phone. She starts to type. I think maybe she's looking it up for me, but suddenly she jabs her phone crossly and pushes it across the table.

'I can't *believe* there's no Wi-Fi,' she says, and bites the head off her Star Bar.

'Oh,' I say. 'Were you trying to look it up?'

She stops chewing and looks at me as if I've only just appeared. Out of the bin. 'Look what up?'

'Whether birds like breakfast cereal?' I say, holding up the cornflakes packet in my hand.

She stares at me, takes another bite of Star Bar, and looks the other way.

'Okay, I'll ask Dad then,' I say.

I go to find him, but I'm not actually sure if he'll tell me either. No one's exactly in a good mood this morning. Except me. Well, I'm sad that Ganda died – I mean, I must be – but I don't mind that we've come to his house, where he used to live. I got to miss a day of school, for one thing. And it was exciting, arriving here really late at night, especially when we realised there was no *bloody electricity*.

My dad said *bloody* a lot last night. He used it for *traffic*, and *hell*, and *all this stuff to sort out* (between *this* and *stuff*.)

Then this morning, he used it for *birds*, because they started tweeting outside the window really early and woke everyone up. And everyone was grumpy because they'd gone to bed really late, because once we'd got here we'd had to shine torches and find candles and blow up airbeds. I thought it was fun, and I didn't mind about the birds either, because I like them, like Ganda did. But I seem to be the only one.

I can't find my dad, so I ask my Aunt Myrna whether birds like breakfast cereal instead. I find her in Ganda's study, picking books up out of a box, looking at them, and putting them back in again. She stops to rub her forehead every now and then, like in an advert for a headache pill.

She looks at me. 'Only for breakfast!' she says. She's smiling but she gets cross the nanosecond I start to say something else. 'We're all very busy today, Archie,' she says without letting me finish. 'Please try not to get in the way.'

So I decide to find out for myself if birds like breakfast cereal.

Of course I know that what they really like is breadcrumbs, but of course there aren't any, because there's no bread. Whenever we came to visit, Ganda would always have a bag of breadcrumbs ready and we'd put them on the bird table in his front garden, and then we'd look through the window to see how many birds came down to eat it. There were always loads of them, and they were always starving.

So they must be really hungry, now that Ganda hasn't been around to feed them for three weeks. So I'm going to feed them, and as there's no breadcrumbs, these cornflakes from a cupboard will have to do.

I was going to ask if I was allowed to go out the front door, but it feels like one of those days when nobody will even notice. So I open the door and step into the front garden.

The garden looks shaggier than I remember it. The last time I'd seen it in daylight was on the day of Ganda's funeral, when everyone came back to his house afterwards for a big party. It was like a birthday party, because people laughed and ate party food, but there was no cake, and the party was for Ganda but he couldn't come. And while I was standing on my own at the party, looking out the window, a lady had come up to me, wearing a big black hat, and she told me that I'd behaved bee-*eautifully* at my grandfather's funeral. For a while she stood with me looking out at the bird table, watching the birds going hop-look-hop-look around the table, with their head tipping this way and that. But when I said, 'Ganda said they move at Charlie Chaplin speed!' she didn't laugh like Ganda used to when he said that. Instead her face folded up a bit, and she squeezed my shoulder really hard, so in the end I said 'excuse me,' and went to get another sausage roll and rub my shoulder. And I thought, I bet no one would've hurt my shoulder like that at a proper birthday party.

The bird table has always stood on the front lawn like a tiny house on a three-legged pole. I walk across the lawn towards it, reaching into the cornflakes packet to grab a handful as I go.

And then I stop.

Because there's something already on the bird table, something quite big, right on the part where the breadcrumbs go.

It's a present.

It's wrapped in silver paper with little white birds on it, and ribbons. I drop my handful of cornflakes and pick it up.

I look back at the house. I think that maybe I'll see my mum, smiling and waving at a window, looking pleased to see me find the little surprise she's put out to keep me amused. But there's nobody at the windows. I hear a *smash* sort of noise from far away inside, and hear my dad call something bloody again. I look back down at the present in my hand, and pull off the silver paper. Inside the wrapping paper is a box, and inside that is a bird. A china ornament bird. It's gold, pink and brown, with a tiny gold beak and bright black eyes.

I stare, wondering what to do with it. I place it on the bird table. The bird's so new and shiny it makes the wooden table look really old and grey. I leave some cornflakes on the bird table, pick up the bird, and take it inside.

*

Mum and Aunt Myrna call everyone down to lunch in Ganda's dining room. They've bought pork pies, apples, and crisps at the village shop. I think it's the best lunch ever and I finish before anyone else. They're all still eating, and nobody's talking, so I decide it would be a good time to make my announcement, since they'll all hear what I have to say.

'I think,' I say in the most grown up voice I can, 'that Ganda gave us a present.'

Nobody reacts in the way that I'm expecting. Everyone's shoulders droop down a bit, and my sister rolls her eyes. No one stops eating.

'Yes, love,' says my mum. 'That's right. He did. He left this *house* to all of us, didn't he, in his *will*. It was a *present*. So we've got to try and sort it all out now, sort out all the – the stuff, in it. That's why we're here, isn't it, love?'

She smiles, and my sister rolls her eyes again. 'Mum, he's nearly eight,' she says. 'You're talking to him like he's a baby.'

'No, Sian,' says my mum, 'no, I'm just explaining things in a way he can understand. This business of wills and bequests can be confusing to the best of us.'

'Calling it a present is actually quite a nice way of putting it!' says Aunt Myrna. She says it with a really big smile but she still looks like she's advertising pills.

I shake my head. 'No,' I say, 'I don't mean the house. I mean, he gave us a present, this morning. He left it on the bird table. And I found it. Here it is.'

I finally have everyone's attention as I reach down and pick up the box, and the wrapping paper, and put them on the table. I feel very grand as all eyes watch me open the lid of the box and put the bird onto the table.

'It's a bird,' I explain. 'I expect he chose a bird because he liked them. And I expect he put it on the bird table because we were all sleeping last night and he didn't want to disturb us.'

No one says anything for a moment. And then my sister snorts.

'Archie,' she says, 'Ganda died –'

'*Passed away*, Sian,' says my mother.

'Okay, well, he passed away weeks ago,' continues Sian. 'How exactly do you think –'

'No,' I interrupt, 'he didn't.' I'm beginning to enjoy the feeling that everyone's listening to my every word. 'Everyone's been saying so. The priest said it at the funeral, and Ganda's friends all said it, and Mum said it loads of times the day that Ganda … passed away. They all said he'd always be with us in spirit. So his spirit must have put the present on the bird table.'

No one is eating any more. My sister rolls her eyes again, but her face looks different from the last time she did it.

In the end, my dad speaks. 'Listen son,' he says, suddenly starting to collect apple cores and crisp packets from the table, 'I expect what's happened is that one of Ganda's friends knew we were coming and left the present for us.' He drains the last of his squash. 'I tell you what, you and Sian can make yourselves useful this afternoon. Go round to all of Ganda's friends in the village to see which one of them left it. Say thank you.'

'Oh, *what?*' moans Sian. 'No!'

'Good idea,' says Mum, standing and beginning to clear the plates. 'I've got their names and addresses in my handbag. It won't take long.'

Sian keeps protesting, but everyone's clearing away now, and no one's listening any more. Uncle Ed is the last one to leave the table, picking up crisp crumbs and putting them in his cup. I want to point out to him that no one would have left us a present because no one knew we were coming; I'd remembered Mum saying that to Dad last night, when Dad complained about the *bloody car* that was parked right in front of the *bloody drive*.

But before I can say anything, Uncle Ed goes off to the kitchen, and then Mum comes and gives us the list of Ganda's friends, telling us to be careful crossing the roads before she turns and goes upstairs.

'Nice going, moron,' snaps Sian.

There are fourteen people on Mum's list. Dad lets me borrow his phone so I can use Google maps to find our way around the village. I tell Sian that I'm going to look at the satellite view and see if we can see ourselves walking round. Sian puts her head in her hands and shouts 'You are such an idiot!' at the pavement, but I think she's really shouting at me.

She walks ahead of me the whole time, except when we have to actually walk up someone's garden path and ring the bell. Then she starts to hang back, as if suddenly I'm the one in charge, so it's always me who has to speak to whoever answers the door.

And after visiting every house, Sian's got something cross to say, like there's no need to hold the present right up into the person's face when I'm talking, and why don't I just throw the bloody wrapping paper away?

In the end I tell her that *she* can do the asking if she wants and that I'm going to tell Mum that she swore. She keeps quiet after that.

And anyway, I don't think how we ask people about the bird would make any difference. Most of them don't recognise us, and they look a bit scared when they open the door. And once they do recognise us, they just look confused when I ask them about a bird on the bird table. One lady doesn't even recognise us when I've told her who we are, and shuts the door saying 'No, not today, thank you,' when I try and ask her about the present.

Only the last lady that we see – the black hat lady who spoke to me at Ganda's funeral – recognises us straight away.

'Oh, it's very nice, isn't it?' she says, when I show her the bird. 'Don't you think so?' She reaches out and takes it from me, gazing down at it in her hands and turning it this way and that. 'And it looks as if it might be rather valuable. It's a wren, I think. Your grandfather loved wrens . . .' For a moment she closes her eyes. 'Now!' she says, opening them again and smiling. 'Won't you both come in for some cake?'

'Oh yes pl– no,' I say, seeing Sian glaring at me.

'No *thank you*,' says Sian, glaring at me again. 'Sorry, we have to get back and help with the house,' she says to the Black Hat Lady.

I know that's a lie and she's not going to help but I don't say anything, even though I would've liked cake.

The Black Hat Lady smiles. 'It's Cherry Madeira,' she says, 'and that was your grandfather's favourite, did you know that? Surely . . .' Her voice suddenly sounds different. '*Surely* they can spare you for five minutes?'

'Um . . . sorry, we have to get back and help with the house,' says Sian again. 'Thank you very much.' She turns to walk back down the path, tugging at my sleeve as she does. At the gate she turns and waves a bit like the queen at the Black Hat Lady who's still just standing and staring at us. 'Thank you very much,' Sian says again. 'Goodbye.' She starts pulling me along by my sleeve and makes me walk super-fast down the path, down the road and round the corner, where Sian slows down.

She takes the bird off me, and looks at it. 'I wonder if it *is* valuable,' she says. She looks at me. 'Are you sure you found this on the bird table?'

'Yes!' I say. Sian doesn't say anything, and gives the bird back to me. We walk the rest of the way back without speaking.

When we get back to Ganda's house I'm pleased to see that the cornflakes I put on the bird table are all gone. We ring the doorbell and Uncle Ed lets us in. The house looks different. There are boxes piled up in the hall, and some of the rooms look naked.

'Hello, you two,' my mum says, as she goes past carrying a box marked *To Oxfam*. 'Well done. Your Uncle Ed's going to get us some fish and chips for tea soon.'

I stand with the bird in my hand, waiting for her to ask me who gave it to us, so I can tell her that nobody did. I realise that my sister is waiting, too. But Mum just carries on walking on through to the front room.

Me and Sian stand there looking at each other for a moment. Then she turns and walks away.

*

We don't use plates when it's teatime because they've all been packed up now, though the adults have glasses for their wine. We just eat our fish and chips out of the paper.

While we eat I wait for someone to ask me about the bird, but nobody does. And in the end it's my sister who says, 'Nobody gave us that bird, you know.'

Everyone looks up from their fish and chips. Sian keeps on eating as she talks. 'Nobody we asked had even seen it before. So it's actually a bit strange, how it got there.'

Everyone looks back down at their fish and chips. They all look a bit like the way my dad looked that time Aunt Myrna didn't realize she'd dropped something on her way to the loo and he'd had to pick it up for her. (I asked but he wouldn't tell me what it was.)

Then my dad speaks.

'Well, perhaps this bird was something that was lost on the street, and then someone else found it and put it on the bird table,' he said. 'So it could be found.'

That didn't make any sense to me. And my mum said, 'That's a bit unlikely, isn't it, Jim? Why would they come all the way into the garden and put it on the bird table? Why wouldn't they just leave it on the garden wall?'

'Well, I don't bloody know, do I?' says my dad. His empty chip paper crunches loudly as he bashes it into a ball between his hands. 'Are you sure you found it on the bird table, son?'

'Isn't it more likely to be just something of Ganda's that was lying round the house somewhere?' Uncle Ed says.

'But I found it on the bird table!' I say. 'I did!'

'And it was gift wrapped, remember?' says my sister. 'So it couldn't have just been something that was lying around. Archie showed you the wrapping paper. He's still got it, haven't you, Archie?'

I just nod. I don't speak, because I'm too surprised that Sian is on my side.

'So don't you think it's just possible,' says Sian, in that same voice she uses when she's telling me ghost stories when we're camping, 'that it was a present from Ganda, after all?'

'*Sian!*' says my mum.

But Sian looks for once like she's enjoying herself.

'What?' she says. 'Think about it. A present, all wrapped in paper with birds on it, appears from nowhere, overnight. And this morning, there it is, waiting for Archie to find when he goes to feed the birds, the way he always used to do with Ganda.'

'Except I had to use cornflakes,' I point out, but Sian ignores me and carries on.

'And then the present turns out to be a valuable ornament – a bird! And Ganda. Loved. *Birds!*'

Suddenly there's a crash, and what looks like blood and diamonds explode all up the wall, and then suddenly the bird flies out of my hand and straight at the wall. There's a loud *crack* and the bird drops onto the floor.

'Dad did NOT give us a bloody present,' Aunt Myrna yells, 'because he's dead, he's bloody *dead*, he's bloody *FUCKING DEAD!*'

For a second nobody moves. And then Aunt Myrna starts sobbing into her hands, and Mum and Uncle Ed rush over and put their arms around her, and Dad stands up, and just stands there.

I rush over to the bird, lying on the carpet. I have to be careful because there are bits of Aunt Myrna's smashed wineglass lying all round it, and the carpet is wet with red wine. I pick up the bird, and my insides turn over when I see that it doesn't have eyes or a beak any more, just a horrible, big scream where its face used to be.

I look around at everyone, and I realise that all the grown-ups are crying. They're not all bawling into their hands like Aunt Myrna, but even just sniffing and wiggling your nose with the back of your hand like my dad's doing is crying. I remember seeing some of Ganda's friends doing it at his funeral. I look over at Sian, and she's just staring at her chip paper and slowly folding its edges with her thumb. I expect her to tut and roll her eyes, but she doesn't, and then without the rest of her face even moving tears start to slide down her cheeks.

I look down at the bird that Ganda's spirit gave us, lying in my hand with an empty space for a face. And I start crying, too.

Aunt Myrna's head comes out of her hands. 'Oh Archie,' she says, 'I'm so sorry!' She comes over and gently takes the bird from my hand. When she looks at it she starts crying all over again, but this time she puts her hand to her mouth, like she's trying to stop the crying from coming out, and she puts her arm round me and hugs me towards her. I feel angry with her for snatching the bird and throwing it but I don't want to look at the bird any more so I bury my face in her side.

She bends over and I watch her pick something up from the floor. 'I'll fix it,' she says, and she's found the bird's face and is holding it on the bird's head, like a mask. 'I'll fix it, and then it'll be good as new.'

She wipes her nose with a tissue and nods when my mum asks her if she's all right. And all the grown-ups are sniffing, and smiling at each other, and blowing their noses. And it feels a bit like those times when we're on holiday in the caravan, when Dad's finished napping and says yes he'll play football now, and Sian says *Me too*, and Mum says she'll make a cup of tea.

My mum comes over. She hugs me and my sister at the same time like we're one big person and gives us both a kiss on our heads. I think she's going to say something about the bird now, but instead she says, 'I bet you two would like some ice cream, wouldn't you? We've bought a box of Cornettos. Do you want to come and get them from the cool box, Sian?'

Sian lifts her eyes from the table and nods, and she goes off with Mum. And I feel better, because I suppose everything's okay now if I'm going to get ice cream.

There's a big splash mark on the wall that's so red my dad could call it *bloody* if he liked, and it wouldn't even be swearing. But although he's sitting and looking at it he doesn't say anything. Mum and Sian come back with the Cornettos and we all eat them without speaking, nibbling and licking, and our heads tip this way and that.

*

It's the next morning, and it's time to leave.

Aunt Myrna walks past with a deflated airbed in her arms. Last night, she handed me the bird, with its face glued back on. It's actually not good as new because it looks different now even though it looks the same. But it's not a horrible scream any more, and that's good.

As she passes me I see her look down at my hands, where I'm holding the bird. She smiles. She looks tired but she doesn't look like she's in a pill advert any more. And just like everyone else she doesn't say anything about where the bird must've come from. Once it got broken the only thing that really seemed to matter was fixing it again so that horrid ugly scream was gone.

I decide to go and say goodbye to the bird table before we go. I walk out to the front garden, and then my heart thudders in my chest. Because the bird table's gone. There are just three lime-green marks on the lawn where its legs used to be.

I can hear my mum and dad talking out in the road, and I run out to tell them. I find them by the car, and they're in the middle of tying the bird table onto the car roof. It looks difficult and keeps slipping.

My dad looks over. 'All right, son?' he says. 'We thought you'd like to take this home, and we can put it in our garden, eh? Then you can feed the birds, just like you used to do with Ganda.' The bird table slips again and I think he's going to start calling it bloody, but he doesn't.

My sister walks past me to the car.

'You can't just keep using cornflakes, you know, Archie,' she says.

'Yes,' agrees my mum. 'We're going to have to think about making some breadcrumbs, aren't we?'

I get into the car, holding onto the bird. And as we drive away, I hold it carefully in my palm and let it look out through the car window.

I show the bird Ganda's house, getting smaller and smaller as we drive down the road. And I show it the Black Hat Lady, who's standing and watching us go past from her upstairs window. And I show it the birds that fly up from a bush as we drive past, and we watch them, both of us. We watch them flying higher. And as the car drives along we're going to keep looking up and watching them, until they're so high that they're not birds anymore; until they're just like tiny breadcrumbs in the sky.

Music and the supernatural – both frequent Fiction Desk themes – come together in this story. See our previous anthologies And Nothing Remains *and* Somewhere This Way *for more of Alastair's work.*

The Ice Cavern

Alastair Chisholm

There was a new girl at the Ice Cavern. She was there for a tryout, and when Davey arrived she was singing an old Cole Porter number, giving it her all. Davey thought perhaps her all wasn't enough; her voice was muddy and lost in the low notes and cracked across the high, making him wince. She was a young girl, in a short denim skirt and yellow T-shirt and high boots, with a piled-up beehive like Ronnie Spector, and between slightly gasping breaths she smiled hopefully towards the back of the room, where William was watching.

Davey ignored her and nodded to William. His brother was dressed in a brown suit and wide striped tie, and he was smoking a cigar and watching the girl with detached enjoyment. Tam the night manager was reporting the bar takings, and William was nodding, but his eyes stayed on the girl. When Davey approached, William waved one hand and Tam left.

'Nice, ay?' he asked, gesturing with his cigar and leaving a question mark of smoke in the air. 'Moira. Nineteen, so she says. Down from the Highlands and all alone ...' He smirked. 'I'll look after her, ay?' He looked across at Davey, and his voice changed. 'You sort things out?'

Davey nodded.

'What'd he say?'

Davey shrugged. 'Said it was a mistake.'

'Aye, a mistake thinking I wouldnae notice two hundred quid going missing.' William glanced around. 'What did you do? You break his legs?'

'Finger.'

'Is that all?' William's face sank in disappointment.

Davey shrugged again. 'That's all it needed.' He thought. 'Held him over the bridge for a bit. He pissed himself.'

William chuckled. 'That's maer like it!'

'He had this,' said Davey, and pulled out a tiny, battered old pistol. His brother leaned back.

'Christ, put that away!' he said, and Davey pocketed it. 'What was that, an old Baby Browning? Haven't seen one o' them since the war.'

The girl on stage stuttered to an end and William put his cigar into his mouth and clapped.

'Lovely stuff, darlin'!' he called. 'Come here, eh? Let's see you.'

The girl came offstage and sauntered towards their table with as much attitude as she could. William looked her up and down. And then again, up and down, and back up. He grinned.

'Aye, that was grand, love. I'm sure we've got a position for you, eh?' He flicked a sly glance at Davey. 'This here's Davey, my brother. Davey, meet Moira.'

The girl blinked her large brown eyes at him, and he nodded, but she'd already turned away. Davey shrugged. He was a large man, heavy shouldered, with thick black hair like moss growing all over him, and a nose broken and reset too often. He was used to the way peoples' eyes flicked to him and then away, as if frightened to rest there.

'Me and Davey, we're business partners,' said William. 'Been doin' this, what, twenty years, now? Aye, twenty years. That's a lot of singers, darlin'. A lot of gorgeous girls, hah!' He laughed, and the girl laughed, though slightly nervously. William put his arm around Davey's shoulders. 'We're a good team, me and him. Brains and brawn. Nae doubt which is which! But Davey here's the talent man. Knows his stuff. Doesnae like the modern bands, Beatles an' that, but all the old singers, old songs, that's him.'

The girl looked at him again, more interested. 'Yeah?' She smiled. 'What did you think of me?'

Davey said nothing, and her expression faltered. William chuckled.

'Dinnae worry doll. Ah don't need Davey to tell me that *you* got some special talent, ay?' He smiled, and the girl relaxed. She gave Davey one more distrustful glance, then turned away and forgot him.

'Aye so,' said William. His eyes gleamed, like they did whenever he saw something he wanted; in the dim lighting they seemed almost black. 'Tell you what, darling, let's go into my office and, ah, get the paperwork sorted, shall we?' He stood. 'Anything else, Davey? About what we were discussing?'

Davey shook his head. 'No.'

'All right then. Come on sweetheart, let's go somewhere more private.' He put his arm around the girl and walked her away, talking and waving his cigar and letting his hand creep down to rest on her bottom.

The bar staff set up tables for the evening. Tam brought Davey a gin and orange and Davey sipped at it. Two other girls were waiting to try out; one was chatting to the pianist, the other standing in shadows behind. It was cool down here in the club, away from the heavy August heat outside, and Davey relaxed, drifting a little to the sounds of bar work, and the tinkle of piano.

After a while, he realised someone was singing, and he looked up. The girl from the shadows had come forward. She wore a pair of old baggy blue jeans and a man's white shirt with the sleeves rolled up. It made her appear frail, like a child. Her feet were bare. Hippy chick. She was singing into the microphone, though it was switched off. The pianist was gone, away having a smoke.

She was singing an old jazz number, *Now Summer's Gone*, a song he hadn't heard for years. She sang alone. She didn't smile to an imagined audience. She sang to the dead microphone, and her voice was the sound of loss.

They'd had some good singers at the Ice Cavern, once. It was a small place, tucked amongst the labyrinthine mess of interconnected rooms under the bridges, but for a while they'd had a reputation. Up and comers, local celebrities, faded stars – Judy Garland had sung there, one evening years ago, still with some of her old glow.

'*The leaves have turned,*' the girl sang, '*and so have you.*'

Her version wasn't the warm, sultry Ella Fitzgerald number, or anything with the jazz of Sinatra, or Billie Holiday's fearlessness. This girl sang as if there was no hope; as if her heart was already broken and the pieces of it were hanging in the air around her, like freezing fog. It was the cold of desolate spaces. Hairs rose on the back of Davey's neck, and the bar staff stopped working and stared. Nobody moved. When they breathed, Davey thought he saw plumes of frost in the air.

At the back of the room, William's office door opened and he emerged, fastening his belt, his mouth open, staring at the stage. The girl ignored him and finished her song. She fell silent and let her head droop.

No-one moved. The barman stood with a glass in one hand, the waitresses stared.

Then William shouted, 'You!'

The girl looked up as if only vaguely interested. She started to walk off the stage.

'Wait! You, there! Sweetheart, what's your name?' William came forward, still tucking his shirt in. Behind him, the office door swung shut.

Now she looked at him.

'Clara,' she said. Her voice was clear as ice, a West coast accent with a pure edge like a silver bell.

'Clara, eh?' William stopped quite close. 'Clara, that was fair something, you know that? Davey, wasn't it?' He turned to Davey, and Davey nodded.

She shrugged and turned as if to walk away.

'Hey! Hey, dunnae go! Clara, you want a job here or not?'

She turned back. 'Doing what?'

There was something about the way she asked. Something knowing, that drove the smirk from William's face for a moment and caused him to stutter.

'Well, I mean. I mean, singing! Doll, wi' a voice like that, don't you want…'

She looked around. Her gaze took in everyone in the club, one by one. As it swept over Davey he felt a shiver inside as if she had left a tiny sliver of ice there.

'I'll sing for you,' she said.

'Eh, aye! Aye, I mean. Well, good.' William was frowning; he didn't understand the way the conversation was going. But he recovered. 'Well, let's go and discuss this somewhere, ah, well mebbes not my office, eh . . . Here, come here, darling, sit here. Ah'm gonna make you a star.'

He drew her to one side and she followed, moving as if pulled on threads. Gradually, the bar returned to life. Davey watched his brother talking, giving the patter, trying to impress. Behind them, a shadow moved hesitantly at the frosted glass door of his office, though no one came out.

Davey finished his cigarette, crushed it into the ashtray with large, careful fingers, and stood up and left.

*

The next day was Friday, and Davey spent the afternoon heaving barrels of beer into the basement. It was hard, physical graft, working alongside hard, physical grafters who respected each other's strength. It was the kind of work Davey liked, but today he was hungover and uneasy. He'd spent the previous evening at home, drinking and smoking and thinking, and his throat rasped. He hawked and spat and kept going, until he was sweaty and his shirt filthy, and finally eased up.

'I'm done,' he muttered, and returned to the bar.

A few customers were there already, but not the big crowd. Still, it was enough for Davey to feel self-conscious in his dirty shirt. He took a bottle and a sandwich and carried it through the back to eat by himself, listening to the crowd through the wall.

At eight, he heard the band starting. He lit a cigarette and poured himself another gin as they crooned, nothing special. At nine, the band stopped, and William's voice cut over the crowd. He was introducing someone, to good-hearted applause. After a minute Davey heard Moira strangling a cover of *Moon River*, and he shook his head.

She managed one more number and then William was back on stage again. There was another trickle of applause, more reserved this time. Then quiet.

Davey sat absolutely still, letting his cigarette hang from his fingers. He waited.

There.

'*The leaves have turned,*' came the voice. '*And so have you ...*'

Clear as a bell, clear as ice, it cut through the air and through the wall and swirled around Davey's head, and he shivered.

'*And summer's warmth has fled, and left me blue.*'

Ash fell from his cigarette, and he didn't move. The small room chilled; frost patterns formed on the inside of his glass, condensation on the walls.

'*You promised love, but now you're gone ...*'

Then he took a single, long, rasping breath, shook the ice from his lungs and lurched to his feet. Stumbling, he pushed out into the club and stared at the stage.

She stood alone in the spotlight, dressed in a simple white shift that glimmered almost silver, feet still bare, eyes closed, hands by her side and shoulders slumped. She looked like she could fall down at any moment, and still the sound poured from her.

With a wrench, Davey looked away and around the room, to the customers at their tables. They stared as he did, mouths open, conversations forgotten. The room was so cold the air almost sparkled.

He saw William, at his usual table. Moira was with him, dressed in black, her face frozen into an unhappy expression, but William was gazing at the stage. Davey noticed that his brother's Brylcreamed hair was grey at the edges, and his skin stretched. He looked old, suddenly. As if his years were outrunning him.

The girl on stage opened her eyes and stared at William, and Davey saw him gasp. Then she turned her gaze on Davey. It was like before, like she was leaving a splinter of ice in his heart; he felt it turning and burning inside him, sharp and so cold he could hardly breathe.

Then the song ended, and she lowered her head, and the room awoke as if from a spell. Guests turned to each other, chuckled, shook their heads. There was applause, but not rapturous – it was as if everyone was slightly bemused. The girl stepped down from the stage.

William was still staring at her. He was smiling with his mouth, but his eyes were black and glittered like frozen tar.

Davey returned to the staff room, poured another gin, and waited. He heard William's voice on stage, and the crowd applauding louder. Then the girl's footsteps down the corridor, to the dressing rooms. And then, after a minute, another, heavier set of footsteps. Davey sighed, and stood up and followed. The door to the dressing room closed as he approached. He hesitated, and then opened it without knocking.

Clara was sitting at the mirror, gazing at her own reflection. William was there, too. He was leaning over her, one hand on her shoulder, the other on the table beside her, blocking any escape. He'd been talking, but she didn't seem to be listening. She wasn't applying make-up, or taking it off, or brushing her hair. She was just . . . looking. William turned as Davey entered.

'Hey, Davey.' His voice was taut. 'What you doing here?'

Davey said nothing.

'Davey? Hello?' William clicked his fingers and grinned. He glanced at Davey's dirty clothes. 'Lookin' a bit rank, brother. Mebbe's need a clean shirt, eh? Hey, ah – me and Clara were just having a wee chat, here. Gie us a bit of privacy, will you?'

Davey said nothing again. He looked at William, into William's black eyes. His brother frowned and chewed his cigar for a moment.

'Davey-boy . . . are you a bit sweet on Clara?' He gave a forced, harsh laugh. 'Is that it? You got a bit of a crush? Clara, you got yourself a puppy dog here. What do you think?'

Clara pulled her eyes away from her own reflection and looked at William in the mirror, and then at Davey, as if she'd only just realised they were there and didn't care much. She gazed at them, and turned back.

Davey stayed where he was, stubborn and stolid. William's smile turned sharp at the corners. He sniffed, nodded, and stood up and away from Clara.

'Well,' he said. 'Well, me and Davey will leave you to it, Clara. Good show, eh? You were . . . I mean –' He shook his head. 'I mean, the audience loves you, darling.'

She said nothing, and William left. As he passed, his eyes crossed Davey's, with a look that Davey knew, and then he was gone.

For a moment, Davey was in the room all alone. All alone with the girl. He moved his mouth into shapes, as if practicing words, but nothing seemed quite right. At last he shrugged.

'I just . . .' He shook his head. 'Sorry.'

He left. There was no sign of William in the corridor.

*

That night, Davey lay in his bed with a splinter of ice turning in his heart. His throat was raw from smoking, but the warmth of every cigarette breath died as it touched the splinter. He'd drunk too much, a half-bottle of whisky taken from behind the bar on the way home and now swirling around his stomach, but its fire was weak and feeble. He shivered and turned and huddled, and when the phone rang he started as if from a nightmare.

The ringing continued. He pulled a hand across his face, tried to clear cobwebs, and picked it up. The plastic of the phone against his forehead was cold.

'Davey.' William. 'You awake?'

'Uh-huh.' Davey looked across at his clock. It was a little after three in the morning.

'I need your help, Davey. At the club, aye? Soon as you can.'

The phone clicked. Davey stared at the wall, thinking. Then he nodded, stood up, and got dressed.

He walked through streets that had forgotten their daytime summer warmth. They glistened in open-skied frost, a blistering cold that turned shadows into blackened edges and stolen knives. He wrapped his leather jacket around him, tucked his hands deep into the pockets and walked with hunched shoulders, and felt as if the tips of his eyelashes were freezing. When he reached the back door to the Ice Cavern it was pitch black. He turned the handle, found it unlocked, and entered.

The lights were off at the back, and in the corridor. He left them off. In the lounge, one lamp glimmered, at William's table. It was freezing cold, terrible cold. There was an empty bottle on the table, and a single glass, and two chairs. One of the chairs was pushed back. In the other sat Clara, gazing dreamily at the lamp as if hypnotised.

Davey frowned.

'Where's William?' he asked. She blinked, and looked up at him, and blinked again.

'Here,' said William, behind him. Davey turned, and coughed as something slid between his ribs. William stared up at him. His eyes were dark and he was sweating, a cold sweat like an addict.

'Here,' he whispered again, pulling out the knife and plunging it back into Davey's chest. This time it stuck, caught on a rib. As Davey lurched, the knife pulled from William's hands.

Davey sat down on the floor in a clatter. He felt suddenly like he'd forgotten how to control his legs, like they were moving without any orders from him. His head waved from side to side.

'.' he said.

William leaned over him, breathing in a ragged, hitched way as if there was something in his lungs he couldn't cough up. He rested a hand on Davey's cheek.

'You shouldn't,' he muttered, as if thinking of something else. 'You shouldn't have stopped me.'

Davey looked up at him and nodded. Then he fired the little Browning pistol through the pocket of his jacket, twice. The first shot punched into William's heart and he fell forward, and the second hit his throat. He collapsed on top of Davey and gave a single retching gasp, and stopped.

Davey lay still. He was growing cold, he realised, and he couldn't feel anything except for the scrape of his breath, in and out. The shots had been muffled by his pocket, and he doubted anyone had heard them outside the club.

Clara shimmered into view. She studied William for a few moments, and smiled. Then she turned back to Davey and stared at him.

Davey nodded.

'Your face is different,' he whispered. 'But I knew it was you.' His lungs were filling with something. 'As soon as I heard you sing, I knew. I remember you.'

She leaned her head to one side and regarded him like an interesting shape on the ground.

'I'm sorry.' He coughed and shook his head. 'I should have stopped him, that time. I should have . . . All the times. I should have stopped him all the times.'

She started to drift away.

'Please!' he called. 'One more.' He coughed again. 'Please.'

She paused, as if considering, and then turned back. Her eyes shimmered, blue and diamond, and she nodded, and sang.

'*The leaves have turned,*' crooned her voice, pure and clear, and Davey sighed. He closed his eyes, let his head rest against the floor of the Ice Cavern, and lay there as she sang, listening until the end.

Toby Wallis makes his first Fiction Desk appearance with this evocative story of personal inertia and national fuel shortages.

The Heart of Everything Young

Toby Wallis

10th September 2000

We stepped out of the front door, into the dense air of late summer, and found a line of stationary cars that reached as far as we could see in both directions. The enormous queue had clogged the whole road, blocking entrances and exits and driveways. No one was getting anywhere.

Sarah and I walked along the side of the road, wondering what was going on. All the drivers seemed tense, glancing in their mirrors at the scale of the queue behind them, or rolling down their windows to lean out and look ahead. We were walking to the petrol station to buy cigarettes and Coca Cola and this was also where the line of cars was heading. As one pulled away from the pumps, the next in line took its spot, and the enormous queue shuffled along behind it. We weaved between them and made our way onto the forecourt. A man filled his car, then took a ten-litre plastic bottle from the boot and started filling that as well. The person in the car behind was upset by this. 'Tanks only,' he shouted. 'Tanks only!'

We bought two litres of Coke and two packets of Marlboro Lights. We couldn't afford such expensive cigarettes but had convinced ourselves we couldn't tolerate anything less. I paid for everything on a credit card I had taken out the year before. The credit company had been steadily raising my limit month by month, and now I had no idea how high it was, or how much of it I had used. We queued in silence, and when we got to the cashier, he asked us which pump we were on.

'No pump,' I said, 'just the Coke and the cigarettes.'

We smoked one each on the way back. The queue was no smaller. There didn't seem to be an end to it. We dodged between the idling cars, the freest people around.

*

In the afternoon, we sat on the sofa, cycling up through the hundreds of television channels I had available, but found nothing of interest. In the end, Sarah gave up and watched a French movie without any subtitles even though she couldn't speak any French, and I read a novel I had taken out of the library. The book was three months overdue but I couldn't pay the fine as the library wouldn't take a credit card.

I had no idea how many television channels I had. We had explored as high as the four hundreds but never found the end of them. My landlord had installed a box which granted me access to all these extra channels after I asked him if he was planning on sorting out the bathroom. There was no flooring in there, just exposed concrete. He was never clear on the legality of the device he attached to the television, and he never fixed the bathroom floor, but to him it seemed a reasonable compromise.

Sarah had wanted to say something about it, but couldn't as she didn't actually live there. She was trying to get a small business started and didn't have a lot of money so she was staying with me in the meantime. A few summers before she had spent a couple of months in Turin and had fallen in love with a particular brand of chocolate biscuit. Now she was planning on starting an import company, buying them in bulk and distributing them to supermarkets around the country. She was certain this was a good idea. Officially I still lived alone as the tenancy agreement was specific in the way it prohibited subletting, but my landlord had become suspicious. He had seen the way our dirty clothes formed a single pile, and the feminine hygiene products that appeared in the bathroom.

'She isn't living here,' I said to him when he pointed these things out. 'We're just sleeping together.'

Sarah, as if on cue, came out of the bedroom wearing only a T-shirt that came down to her knees. My landlord seemed satisfied with that.

We were not sleeping together. We were only sharing the bed. At first, she had slept on the sofa using an unzipped sleeping bag for a blanket, but I felt guilty and offered to switch with her. The sofa was too short for me to lie comfortably, and the wooden supports dug through the cushions and into my ribs.

'Let's just share the bed,' she said one morning as I tried to stretch out my neck and lower back. So we slept in the same bed keeping to our own sides, being careful to make sure that no part of ourselves ever touched.

When the film finished, Sarah went to the bathroom and I got up and set the channel back to one. The news was on. Gridlocked cars queued outside petrol stations across the country. Trucks formed slow-moving roadblocks on the motorways. Picket lines had formed outside petrol refineries and distribution centres. On the bottom of the screen was the word *crisis*.

'There's a crisis,' I called out to Sarah.

'When are you going to get some fucking floor tiles in here?' she called back.

11th September 2000

A sign appeared on the garage forecourt saying there was now a five pound limit per customer. I saw it on my walk to work. The number of cars coming and going had reduced, but there was still a steady flow of them. I wasn't sure how the garage staff would police this five pound limit. How they would stop people taking more.

The petrol crisis was caused by a dispute over the taxation of fuel. The images on the front of the newspapers seemed underwhelming. Truck drivers formed a protest group and blockaded the entrances of the refineries. It didn't seem to have much of an effect at first, but steadily more drivers joined the effort, and soon it was as though they had tied a tourniquet around an artery.

At work, there had been two delivery lorries scheduled, but only one came. We weren't even sure if that one was going to turn up. I was almost disappointed when it did. Chris and I dragged the stacked pallets of food out onto the supermarket floor, and the shelf stackers were told to spread things out a bit to make it look not quite as bad as it was. The whole job took about an hour less than usual. Everyone stood around, talking in little groups, filling in the time.

When it was almost nine, I stood at the entrance to the supermarket holding the keys to the door. On the other side, a small crowd had gathered, waiting for us to open. I was not supposed to unlock the door before nine am. The people outside showed me their watches, becoming more agitated.

'Look at him,' an old man said, 'he's enjoying his little bit of power.'

And he was right. I was enjoying it. At two minutes past nine I unlocked the door and let them in.

After opening the supermarket, Chris and I were supposed to go around emptying the bins and gathering up the trolleys, but we tended to go back to the warehouse and into the walk-in freezer instead. The freezer was set to minus eighteen degrees Celsius and you had to wear padded thermal jackets plus big gauntlets and hats that made movement difficult. It was an uncomfortable place to be, but a good way to avoid being asked to do anything.

Chris and I were in there playing catch using a tennis ball we had found, throwing it the full length of the room. The thick jackets and gloves made throwing the tennis ball hard, and our efforts were frequently off-target. We spent most of the time scrabbling around, trying to pull the ball out from under the racking. Outside, the weather was fine, but in there our breath fogged and our toes went numb inside our safety boots.

We listed jobs we would prefer to be doing as we passed the ball back and forth. Chauffeur. Milkman. Locksmith. None of the jobs were so extravagant, none of them technically out of our reach. Grounds-keeper. Cinema projectionist. Nightwatchman. The fact that these ordinary jobs were not ours left us feeling worse, as though we were less than failures.

Chris made a bad throw and it was impossible to catch. I didn't even try. The ball knocked a shelf off its hinges and scattered dozens of boxes of fish fingers across the floor. They were hard to pick up in our massive gauntlets. We put the badly dented ones toward the back.

*

Sarah and I watched the news on television. The petrol crisis was worsening. Six refineries and four distribution centres had been blockaded, but mainly people didn't seem to mind. Public support was strong. Reporters stopped people on the street and told them they were two days away from running out of fuel entirely, but everyone seemed to shrug it off as though they didn't think this would be such a problem.

'What's this going to do to my import company?' Sarah said. 'Have they considered that?'

All the protesters seemed calm, softly spoken, and measured. They were clear in what they wanted and in holding out until they got it. It all seemed perfectly reasonable.

'I don't expect they will think the biscuits are important,' I said.

We knew it was serious when the queen got involved. Tony Blair asked for emergency powers, which she granted, and it felt like a finely crafted twist closing the second act of a play. It was the best thing on television by far.

That night we were woken by a hammering sound. We sat up in bed, confused, a space between us large enough for a third person, each wearing a T-shirt that belonged to me. My neighbour's front door was right next to my bedroom window, and her boyfriend was knocking loudly. It sounded like he was using the side of his fist, and he called out to her while he was doing it.

'Let me in, Laura,' he shouted, over and over.

Laura had locked him out again. I looked at the clock and saw that I had two hours and fifteen minutes until I needed to get up for work. His voice had the strained hum of an old lawnmower, fibrous and wet like he needed to cough something up.

'Shut up!' Sarah shouted. 'Laura doesn't love you anymore.'

The hammering stopped and for a moment there was silence. Then he began crying, sobbing gently on my neighbour's doorstep. We listened to him for a while.

'I feel bad,' Sarah whispered to me after about five minutes.

'You should,' I said.

12th September 2000

Traffic disappeared completely. There wasn't a single car on the barren roads. The five pound limit sign had been replaced by one saying that the pumps were dry. Traffic cones stopped people from driving onto the forecourt. I worried that the whole place was closed and I wouldn't be able to get my cigarettes, but it was open. Inside, the cashier was playing on a Nintendo Gameboy and seemed to resent having to put it down to serve me.

It was weird having no traffic around. Everyone's cars were parked on their driveways, preserving what little fuel people had. Everything seemed still. I walked down the middle of the road like I was the last man on earth. Like it all belonged to me.

When I arrived at work, I discovered that Chris no longer worked at the supermarket. For a moment, I worried he had done what we had been dreaming of and found a job cutting grass or putting little stickers onto the sides of fruit, but he hadn't. He had been fired for stealing food. They caught him leaving with a dozen trays of sushi in his rucksack. I was annoyed because it meant I would have to unload the deliveries by myself, but it didn't matter because no deliveries came. We all stood around wondering what we were supposed to do and when the store manager came out, we figured he would tell us, but he stood there wondering what to do as well. A small crowd gathered at the entrance to the supermarket, but this time they weren't waiting for us to open. They were pressed up against the glass, trying to see how bad it was.

I spent the afternoon in the freezer by myself.

*

When I got home, Sarah had shaved all her hair off. She was sat on the sofa, reading a book about business strategy and looked up at me as I walked in. I hardly recognised her. Her face seemed smaller. Her ears bigger. It had changed the whole shape of her head.

'I've made a mistake,' she said.

Inspired by the cost-effectiveness of buying a set of clippers and never going to the hairdressers again, she had decided to trim her hair short, but there had been a mix-up with the attachments, and all further attempts to neaten or disguise what had happened had led to an ever-shortening of what remained. There was now as good as nothing left.

With her glasses on, she looked post-detox serious. Like someone who had been through some stuff and come out the other side, calm and enlightened.

'I think you look good,' I said.

Sarah studied herself in the bathroom mirror, standing barefoot on the cold concrete floor, tilting and angling her head.

'I don't hate it,' she said.

We sat on the sofa with an ashtray between us, watching the news. The discussions between the government and the protestors were gripping, both sides making impossible demands of the other. The protestors wanted guaranteed price cuts and limits on tax increases. The government demanded they pack up and walk away. Both sides argued this was a problem for the other to resolve. It was hard to see how it could end. There was a tension that hummed behind every interview. A fragility had been exposed. What else might happen? What else could break?

13th September 2000

When I arrived at work, the manager stopped me as I was coming through the door.

'You don't work here anymore,' he said.

I assumed I had been discreetly fired for all the time I had wasted hiding in the freezer. That they had initiated, progressed, and concluded the full HR disciplinary process without feeling the need to mention it to me. I felt like a character in a Kafka novel.

'But why?' I said, trying to sound bewildered and innocent, wondering if I would be able to argue a case. I imagined CCTV footage of me standing motionless in the freezer for an hour and then quietly conceded the legitimacy of their point. But that wasn't it.

'Your contract expired,' the manager said. 'Your last day was yesterday. Six months fixed term. Did you read the paperwork?'

I had not. All I could do was walk away.

Later that morning, I stopped in the library to update my CV. The computers were occupied, so I walked around, browsing for something to read. I selected a horror novel with an exciting cover and sat where I could see the computers so I would know when one was free. The horror novel didn't hold my attention. I read about twenty pages of it before giving up and setting it down. On the wall was a flyer looking for someone to join a barbershop quartet, and for a moment I actually considered it.

When one of the computers became available, I retrieved my CV from an old email I had sent to myself. There wasn't a great deal on it. I had already increased the point size to help it fill two pages. I added a new line at the top of the job history section. It said:

Warehouseman, Mar 2000 – Sep 2000

One of the librarians was pushing a trolley up and down the stacks, placing books back on the shelves. She had a pair of glasses pushed up on her head, which she dropped over her eyes any time she needed to check the Dewey Decimal codes on the spines. I felt like this was precisely the kind of job I was looking for. I was certain I could do it, but at the same time, I was certain they would not let me.

I deleted the word *warehouseman* and replaced it with *warehouse operative*.

*

At home I found a letter on my doormat. It was an electricity bill. Without looking at how much I owed, I put it on top of the fridge, which was where I put things I knew were important but that I preferred to ignore.

Sarah was sat on the floor in front of the television. She was wearing one of my hoodies and had an ashtray on the floor in front of her.

'Have you seen this?' she said, gesturing at the television. Cigarette ash spilled onto the carpet.

Petrol reserves were now rationed to critical emergency services. Police escorts were being given to tankers that the protesters made an exception for, making sure ambulances and fire engines were stocked. Doctors and nurses had to present hospital ID to buy the fuel that had been made available to them, but it still wasn't enough. Blood supplies to hospitals had been interrupted. The public mood was shifting as people imagined waiting for an ambulance that wasn't coming. Some people had crossed the English Channel into France in the hunt for fuel. Shops had run out of fresh food, and those with sufficient foresight had been panic buying whatever they could get.

I went into the kitchen and started digging through the cupboard, seeing what food I had available. It wasn't much. Some packets of dried noodles, a box of colourful breakfast cereal, a couple of days' worth of Coke. In the fridge was an old pint of milk that had started to separate. I pulled my shoes back on and Sarah and I went to the shops and bought whatever we could get. It wasn't much. We came away with two carrier bags filled with tubes of Pringles, assorted chocolate bars, and some breath mints. It all went on the credit card.

*

I woke in the night to the sound of my neighbours having sex. Laura had forgiven him for some reason. The bed banged against the wall arrhythmically. Every now and then, they called out each other's names in a passionless facsimile of the kind of sex they thought they ought to be having.

I sat up in bed and saw that Sarah, still wearing my hoody, was asleep. I got out of bed and tripped on a pile of our laundry, but she didn't wake up.

In the kitchen, I poured a large glass of water, took it into the living room, and sat down in front of the television. I cycled up through the channels, looking for something to watch, but I didn't know what I wanted to see. I skipped through them, barely stopping to give anything a chance. When I found a channel showing a pornographic film, I decided that would do and lay down on the sofa. The film was set in a bicycle shop. It was hard to imagine who its target audience was. In the distance I could still hear Laura and her boyfriend having sex, flatly declaring each other's names.

When I woke up, the pornography had finished and been replaced with a shopping channel selling The World's Sharpest Knife. The man on the screen demonstrated the knife by slicing a Coke can in two.

14th September 2000

Sarah didn't even think to ask why I wasn't at work. For a moment, I was annoyed by how little attention she paid to me, but then I reminded myself, we aren't together, we're just sharing a bed. I took a shower, and when I came out Sarah was cross-legged on the sofa eating Pringles and listening to music with a big pair of headphones on. I stood in the doorway and mouthed the words *I'm going out*, and she gave me two thumbs up and mouthed the word *okay*.

The petrol station was fully closed now. All the lights were off, the door was locked. I took out my cigarettes and counted how many I had. Eight. I started doing calculations, figuring out how long they would last, how best to ration them. I smoked the first immediately.

The queue in the job centre was long, and the waiting area was crowded. There was a sign up saying the petrol crisis had led to staff shortages and waiting times would be longer than usual. There was brooding anger running through the whole place, but it was always like that to some extent.

I didn't join the queue. I stood in front of the vacancies boards, scanning down to see what jobs were available. Few appealed to me. Event planner, salesman, call centres. No one was looking for me. They used phrases like *high energy* and *good communicator* and *fast-paced environment*. I could feel the anxiety rising in me as I read them.

I walked out of the job centre without having spoken to anyone. I figured I would go back in a few days. There didn't seem any hurry. I didn't want to go home, so I wandered in and out of the shops, reading the backs of paperback novels like I might buy one, or browsing the homeware sections like a cafetière or a handheld vacuum cleaner was just what I needed.

In the newsagent's I saw the headlines on the newspapers. They said the petrol crisis was over. Some kind of agreement had been reached and the blockades had been lifted. The protestors said they were giving the government sixty days to make improvements, or they would do it all again. I was disappointed. It didn't seem like much of an ending, as if the credits had started rolling halfway through the movie. I flipped through the newspaper, but there wasn't a lot of detail. They said it would take several days for things to return to normal, like the slow return of blood to a numb limb, but as unexpectedly as it had started, it was over.

'This isn't a library,' the woman behind the till said to me. I put the newspaper down and left.

Walking home, I took a detour through a multi-storey car park. I don't know why. There were a few cars dotted around, but it was mostly empty. I walked up the ramps, spiralling around the car park until I made it to the roof. I leaned against the railing, lit the second of my remaining cigarettes, and looked out over the town. The roads were empty. Everything was still and quiet. The only movement I could see were the trees blowing in the gentle wind and the slow motion clouds as they drifted from shape to shape.

*

In the evening I waited for Sarah to go to bed, then retrieved the electricity bill and dialled the twenty-four-hour automated payment line. I listened to the instructions all the way through, then entered my card details. The cheerful pre-recorded message asked me to wait while they processed the payment. I looked out of the living room window. There were no stars in the sky. Only light pollution. My card was declined. I listened to a new part of the message I had never heard before. The tone of voice was different. It sounded apologetic but judgmental. I was invited to press one and try another payment method. I hung up the phone.

I went out onto the front porch, sat on the lawn chair, and smoked the last of my cigarettes. Because it was the last, I tried to pay attention to it as I smoked. On the other side of the road, a fox was digging through a bin bag. Behind a closed curtain the blue light of a television flickered. I felt settled and calm, like I had fallen in a well, landed, and could take a break before figuring how I was going to climb back out.

From off in the distance, I heard the sound of a car. It took me a moment to realise it was the first I had heard in a while. The sound of the engine was noisy and intrusive, and when it got close, it drove past going faster than it should have been. Its tyres skidded and the engine roared. The fox startled and ran away, and I watched the rear lights of the car as it careened away into the darkness. I had finished my cigarette before the sound disappeared.

15th September 2000

The petrol crisis disappeared from the news. Even though the protesters had made it clear that if the government didn't take action they would return and do it all again, no one believed they would. The blockades moved on, and the tankers got back on the roads. With the news no longer interesting, we watched the opening of the Olympic games in Sydney. The athletes marched their flags around the stadium, all so happy to be there. I sat cross-legged on the sofa with the local free newspaper, using a pen to circle jobs I might be able to do.

'What about that one?' Sarah said, pointing indiscriminately at the page. I shook my head.

'It says you need RTITB accreditation.'

The athletes from North and South Korea marched together under a unified flag. Everyone clapped and smiled.

'How do you get that?' she said. 'Do you just have to send away for the certificate?'

I turned the page.

In the afternoon, my landlord popped in. I tried to explain about my job and how I might not be able to pay the rent on time, but he didn't seem too bothered. He had a special radio that could tune in to police frequencies and was excitedly showing it to us. Sarah asked him about the bathroom floor, but he pretended not to hear.

'You can listen in, but you can't talk back,' he said. 'But you probably shouldn't do that even if you could. This thing isn't strictly legal. Do you mind if I leave it here? Don't tell anyone you have it.'

We put the radio away in a cupboard and lost all interest in it.

*

I went back to the library to print out copies of my CV and ended up staying there till it closed. Walking home, the roads were a little busier. Now that the crisis had been resolved, people were happy to drive, confident that they could get more fuel anytime they wanted it. I walked past the petrol station and instinctively reached to my pocket for a cigarette, but I didn't have any. People went inside to pay for their fuel, but I kept walking, no space on the credit card for anything.

When I got back, Sarah was on the lawn chair, cross-legged like a yogi. She was wearing big, plastic sunglasses that I had never seen before. She waved at me as I got close.

'Come and see this,' she said, and led me inside.

In the centre of the living room were five hundred boxes, each containing twenty-five individually wrapped Italian chocolate biscuits. They had been stacked into a neat oblong. I walked around it, admiring the brick-like construction.

'They arrived this morning,' she said.

'For your business?' I said.

Sarah lifted the sunglasses up onto her smooth head. She looked strong, like someone from a Richard Kern photograph.

'I ordered them a while ago,' she said, 'but I guess with everything, it took a long time to get them here.'

I folded my arms and stood back. I was impressed. She had actually managed to do something.

'Can I try one?' I said, picking up one of the boxes. All the writing on it was in Italian. I couldn't read a word. She took the biscuits from me and put them back on the pile.

'Sorry,' she said, 'I need them for the business.'

'So, what are the next steps?' I said. 'How do you progress from here?'

Sarah lifted one finger to her lips, looked at the stack of boxes, and then out of the window. She didn't say anything. I could hear cars passing on the road outside.

We sat down on the sofa and looked at the television across the top of Sarah's new inventory. We cycled up through the channels, climbing higher and higher. Six hundred, seven hundred, eight hundred, there didn't seem to be an end to it.

Some borders are easily identified, thanks to the presence of a high wall, a curt sign, or a sudden abundance of peaked caps and automatic weapons; others you're not aware of until you realise that you've already crossed them. This is Zeph Auerbach's first Fiction Desk story.

Desynchronisation at Seven Sisters

Zeph Auerbach

Before I get into it, I want to explain that Ed and I had already been drifting apart for some time. We were both twenty-four when events were set in motion. We both had long-term girlfriends (mine was a fiancée). He lived in North London; I lived in South London. I already had a sense that, like other friends, he'd grown to care about things that I didn't – job progression, interior design, posh restaurants – things that hadn't mattered to us as boys. I guess I'd sort of assumed we'd made an unspoken promise we would never care about those things, but for him this was just part of growing up. The natural course of things.

So that's how it was already, whenever I hung out with Ed and Charlie and the others: I felt left out (which wasn't their fault), and like I couldn't really keep up with them, and maybe I should've grown up better, instead of staying fixated on childish things like videogames and pizza buffets and *what ifs* and *would you rathers* and *what would you dos*.

When Ed and I were teenagers, we'd use up a whole weekend just like that. Making silly videos, playing GoldenEye, pulling pranks on each other, inviting everyone else over for a kick around in the shitty little park near my house, eating huge quantities of pasta, staying up late in the front room so we could try to watch softcore porn on Channel 5 and having to switch the channel over when my suspicious mum walked in.

And like I say, even before this thing started, it already wasn't like that anymore. I know that.

I wish I had just one photo of Ed. I tried to draw him recently, from memory. It looked nothing like him.

There's no way of telling this to you in a way that doesn't sound crazy. This is probably why it's taken me years to actually type it out.

It happened twelve years ago.

I was going to meet Ed at Seven Sisters underground station before walking over to Charlie's. We'd done this a hundred times before; it was mundane. I'd always get a huge, cheap bag of crisps at a newsagent's by the station, and Ed would get the fanciest chocolates he could find. Gifts to the host that I would almost singlehandedly consume. We'd walk the fifteen or so minutes to Charlie's whilst catching up on football and friends and work (in that order).

We didn't really have a standard meeting spot at Seven Sisters, which was unfortunate because there were three main exits: a side exit on Seven Sisters Road, one weird one that comes up on the other side of Tottenham High Road, and one in the middle between the other two, that I always found hard to find. It bugs me even now that we didn't have a standard meeting spot; we were used to getting above ground and sorting things out by texting or waving at each other, and then even if we had to faff about a bit to find each other we never had enough reason to improve our system for next time.

Anyway. I think I came out at the side exit and I texted Ed (I still have all these texts saved): AT THE SIDE EXIT. YOU HERE? No response for a while. I considered going to get snacks, but I decided against depriving him of that experience, so I wandered over to the middle exit. From there you can see the weird exit across the road too. No sign of him. Whatever. I texted my mum while I waited – a couple of :) :) in response to a joke from the internet she was sharing around.

Then I got a text from Ed: HERE. WHERE ARE YOU? Great, I thought, I'll do a sweep of the exits. He wasn't at the middle exit. I couldn't make him out across the road at the weird exit. So I walked around to the side exit, but he wasn't there. Maybe he'd texted me a bit earlier and he'd had poor reception so the message had been delayed – maybe he'd gone to buy snacks without me, the bastard. I nosed around a few of our favourite newsagents'. Nope.

Right, back to trying each of the exits. I texted him: COOL, I'M HERE – I'LL GO TO THE WEIRD EXIT ACROSS THE ROAD.

He replied: I'M HERE.

I'm here isn't the greatest of texts, but I took him to mean the weird exit. But he really wasn't there, so I thought maybe he took the side exit to be the weird exit, so I trotted back there, but he still wasn't there, and I was quite frustrated and sighing quite heavily at this point. (Why hadn't we just established an unambiguous meeting point? You should've seen how much fun we used to have meeting up at Bank station, which has nine exits.)

Then he texted me: I'M STANDING RIGHT HERE, BY EXIT 2, BUS STOP K. BY SOME TEXAS BEST CHICKEN PLACE.

I didn't know these reference points, so I checked the side exit and then the middle exit, but they didn't match, which only left the weird exit. So yes, he had meant the weird exit. I still couldn't see him, so I crossed the road, which involved taking the pedestrian subway from the middle exit to the weird exit, and I remember feeling relieved, as I jumped down the first set of steps and then leapt up the next set of steps, that we were finally done with this awful, tedious hassle. But then I looked all around: Exit 2, Bus Stop K, Texas Best Chicken – but no Ed. Was he pranking me? I'd been the victim of some pretty dire pranks of Ed's over the years, but this would've taken the biscuit.

I rang him up. I was fully prepared to tell him that he wasn't being funny and call him a fucker. But I got a female computer voice telling me, 'That number is not recognised,' which was strange. He texted: I'M RIGHT HERE. BUS STOP K. IS THIS ONE OF YOUR SHIT PRANKS? I literally searched around that bus stop like we were playing hide-and-seek (Was he crouching behind the bin? Was he hiding in an old lady's trolley?). I was starting to get scared, though I wouldn't have admitted that to him, even if I'd found him. I ran down the subway and up to the middle exit and then I ran around to the side exit, before running back to the weird exit, to where he said he was, but he wasn't there.

I entertained all sorts of ludicrous notions, like maybe I'd lost the ability to distinguish faces. Maybe someone had mis-labelled the bus stop signs and tube exits as some sick anarchic joke. I rang him up and got the same female computer voice telling me, 'That number is not recognised.'

I texted him: I'M HERE AT EXIT 2, BUS STOP K, ACROSS THE ROAD FROM THE MAIN STATION, JUST OUTSIDE TEXAS BEST CHICKEN.

SO AM I, he replied.

I'm not usually fazed by the hustle and bustle of London streets, but at that point I seriously wanted to switch it all off – just switch off the excruciatingly noisy people and cars and buses, leaving me and Ed to hug in the awkward way we always did.

What would you have done in that situation? Would you have kept looking? And for how long? Me, I was there for over forty minutes. I have text messages between us spanning the whole time. I was terrified. I had no idea what was happening. I felt like I must've been losing my mind. You know when you've just woken up from a nightmare and you can't shake that hazy dread that sits on top of your lingering illogical thoughts?

In the end I texted him: I DON'T KNOW WHAT'S HAPPENED. I'LL GO TO CHARLIE'S. I'LL SEE YOU THERE. No awkward hug. No crisps, no chocolates. No catching up on football and friends and work. I walked in a daze. I kept looking about myself, expecting to see Ed's wonky smile looming towards me.

I've never seen Ed again.

By the time I was walking up to Charlie's door, I was in a state of shock.

Then I received a text from Ed, saying: I'M NEARLY AT CHARLIE'S. WHAT'S HAPPENING? PLEASE 100% PROMISE ME YOU ARE NOT MESSING WITH ME.

I texted him back: I PROMISE. I'M JUST ABOUT AT CHARLIE'S. ED, I'M SCARED.

ME TOO.

When I opened the door and saw wonderful Charlie – normal, solid, three-dimensional Charlie – I gave him a warm, non-awkward hug and held on to him for a long time. He asked me, 'What's wrong?' and I explained everything. I just couldn't stop talking. I went over all the details about the different exits and I was gasping for breath and pacing the front room of his small flat and then he went silent for a while and then he said, really flat and cold, clearly scared himself:

'Who's Ed?'

My God, this hit me harder than anything. This was Charlie; it was always me and Charlie and Ed.

'Ed . . . *Ed!*' I shouted. There was no point refreshing his memory with anecdotes and whatnot – Charlie *knew* Ed, had known him since he'd been eleven, since we'd met on Platform 2, Hartesmere East station, on our first day to school.

'Mate, I don't know what you're talking about,' Charlie said. 'You mentioned an Ed when you texted me, but I thought that was a typo.'

I left. It would be a couple of days before I'd be able to stomach talking to Charlie again.

*

As I left Charlie's, the only thing keeping me a little bit reassured was that I was still receiving texts from Ed.

CHARLIE HAS NO MEMORY OF YOU. NONE. WHAT THE ACTUAL FUCK IS THIS? COME OVER TO MINE.

I staggered back to Seven Sisters, still believing I would see him at any moment, feverishly texting him and feeling such relief every time I got a reply.

I now keep an archive of all our texts. It's over 800,000 words.

At Seven Sisters I felt taunted by those exits – the weird, the middle, the side, the middle, the side, the weird – that had somehow juggled Ed out of existence. And I was scared to go underground, because going underground meant messing with the phone's reception, and that was my only link left to Ed. What if plunging to the depths meant I'd lose him forever?

We soon discovered that our phones were the only things tethering us to one another. This was 2008 and they were brick phones (already outdated – fashionably? – at the time). We could only text. Emoticons but no gifs.

There was no Ed at Ed's flat. There were three girls – strangers – who thought I was well odd.

I phoned my mum before I phoned Bethany, my fiancée. Then my mum phoned Bethany before I had a chance. They were concerned for me. They had no concern at all for Ed, because *Who's Ed?*

My mum used to do some of Ed's washing for him when he stayed over. She's the one who cooked us the huge quantities of pasta. She would've adopted Ed in a heartbeat. Now, just: *Who's Ed?*

It would be a few weeks until I managed to track down Ed's parents, Tony and Fi, and even though they didn't recognise me, I convinced them I was an old friend and they helped me find the flat where he lived, which wasn't in London, where it should've been, but in Reading, and I lurked outside until this man came out who looked like Ed but wasn't, hanging out with a woman I didn't know, and twin toddlers. I texted Ed but this man – with all the dimensions of Ed and the gait of Ed and that wonky smile of Ed's, but none of it convincingly Ed – didn't touch his phone, while I got a message in reply, from the real Ed, not this imposter. I couldn't bring myself to say hi, because what would I have said? He didn't know me and I didn't know him. So I slipped away. I've never returned.

I've often thought about how that 'Ed without me' seemed pretty happy and successful. Like, having me torn out of his past clearly didn't fuck him up.

Ed and I have never been able to work out exactly when our worlds desynchronised from each other. We say that we desynchronised at Seven Sisters, but we've deduced it probably happened a couple of weeks before that. Some of the things we'd texted just hadn't quite matched up.

For instance, we'd been watching a football game in our separate flats: Liverpool (my team) vs. Arsenal (Ed's). And we'd been texting each other throughout. We did this occasionally and I was more into it than him, to be honest; I think he kept up following Arsenal partly for my sake. So when Torres scored in the first ten minutes I rubbed Ed's face in it: LOOKS LIKE YOU'RE GOING TO GET QUITE THE BEATING. Then he replied, 'EH? WHAT?' At some point towards the end of the first half, when Arsenal were just passing the ball in their half, he texted, ARKANO! ARKANO! COULDN'T YOU JUST KISS HIM? which struck me as bizarre. There wasn't even a player called Arkano in the Arsenal team. Then he texted, YOU'LL NEVER COME BACK! when *we* were 2-0 up. It all felt a bit eerie. However, the notion hadn't occurred to me that we could be watching entirely different games; instead I'd assumed Ed was trying out a bold, ironic sense of humour. I later found out that he'd assumed the same about me.

Things didn't go back to normal with Charlie. He promised me he believed me. He pretended. But I couldn't shake the feeling that he treated me differently. Warily. I noticed he made a point of smiling when he saw me, but I could tell that I was a chore for him.

Bethany never really understood. She tried. I honestly think that she tried to share in my delusion, as she saw it. She tried to get to know Ed. Ed tried from his side too. There was a lot of *Ed asks this* and *Bethany asks that.* But there must've always been this niggling feeling for her that this was just a phase. Ed was just some strange internet friend, some sci-fi roleplay game gone too far. She wanted to get married and have kids. Things dissolved.

I've never told anybody else. I don't want to be a figure of fun. I don't want to be studied. I don't want to be a five-minute clickbait vid.

By the point Bethany left, it was already hard for me to stay in regular contact with Ed. The irony is that we were never great over text. I mean, look at the texts I've quoted here. They're hardly Byron and Shelley, are they? We were faces people. Awkward hug people. PS3 headset people. We liked to make each other laugh and hear the laughter. Aside from the occasional football match commentary, our texts were for basic admin or throwaway gags.

Our PS3s did not connect to the same servers. Our football seasons diverged. The news from my world no longer had any meaningful relationship to the news in Ed's world. We had no photos or recordings whatsoever of each other; they'd vanished. My memory of Ed's laugh grew more distant, muffled.

Like I said, I tried to draw him but I couldn't.

A few years passed. I think I was the last person left in London in their twenties with a brick phone. It became cracked and scratched and buggy. I tried to get it fixed but the guy in Dr Phones UK didn't understand. *Why keep that thing? Why not upgrade? Look, this one has 4G.*

Yes, but it doesn't have my disembodied Ed, who has diverted to a timeline where we never met, does it?

So I held out as long as I could before getting a smartphone. After Bethany left, I realised my other friendships were withering away too. Modern culture does not tolerate a brick phone. Modern culture does not tolerate an obsessive recluse. Of course I kept my brick too. But I bought another phone: faster and shinier, with the promise of socially warmer times. I tried to keep up with the groupchats and make friends with colleagues at work with shared interests, but it all felt like I was cheating on Ed.

We promised each other that we would try to 'move on', as it were, and commit to our other friends. But it was Ed and me who had gone through this thing together and nobody else was ever going to understand.

The years dragged on. I kept my brick on my bedside table and I tried to message him every night, even if it was something complete inane. Then once every other night. I knew it was hard for him too. We'd been through the most spectacular and unique disruption of space-time together but we barely had anything left to say to each other.

Sometimes Ed wanted to talk about job progression and interior design and posh restaurants, and I did my best to sound interested.

I had a meltdown when the charger for my brick phone broke and I was scared that I wouldn't be able to find a replacement, or that even if I did it wouldn't work, and it'd be like in an action movie where Ed's fallen off a cliff, and I'm trying to hold on tight to his hand but his fingers are slowly slipping away.

In the end I managed to get a charger (in fact I got four, just in case).

Ed's gotten married and has had a kid. So have I. I want to tell my wife, Georgia, all about Ed, but I daren't. In the future I'll be desperate to tell my daughter, Rebecca. But I won't.

My brick now resides in a shoebox under my side of the bed. I get it out every weekend (or every other). Sometimes Ed hasn't texted at all. Sometimes Ed has reminded me of something we did together long ago that I'd forgotten.

I live in an old cobalt Nokia 3310 in a shortbread tin in Ed's T-shirt drawer. He told me.

If one day I don't receive any more messages, what am I to assume? There are too many blanks to fill in. A crossword setter, a Sudoku designer, a mystery writer – they all make you a promise: you will have enough information to solve this. It's not like that.

In the first few years, we used to arrange to go to the same place, like the top of Brockwell Park, and look out together over London. Once we both went to the bench at the end of the shitty little park near my old family house, where we used to play football, and we drank beers by ourselves while we reminisced over texts. We stopped all that a while ago. I think we'd find it too hard now.

I haven't mentioned something to Ed: I have a new friend from work now, called Raph. We've joined a Saturday football team. Sometimes, even when we're knackered from work and childcare, we stay up until silly hours playing Fortnite together. We send each other animated gifs and funny videos. He's a Spurs fan.

What's in a naming? The answer is many layers of conflict and tension, according to this first Fiction Desk story from Southampton writer Andrew Cochrane.

Name

Andrew Cochrane

'I'm afraid you cannot name your child that.'

There was a desk fan over the man's shoulder, on top of a filing cabinet. It rattled as it swept left and right. There were brown stains on its base, as though coffee had been spilled on it and so it had been moved off the desk and out of the way.

'Excuse me?' she said.

In saying this she clutched the baby closer to her chest, as though to prevent the man leaning over the desk and taking him.

'We cannot allow this name to go through,' the man said.

'Nikos,' she said, looking sideways at the father. He only sat back in his chair and lifted his hands out of his lap for a moment, palms facing the ceiling.

'Nikos,' she said again, firmly this time.

He sighed and leant forward.

'Why not?' he asked the man behind the desk.

'You cannot name your child that,' the man said.

Nikos looked at Renata and then back at the man.

'That is not a why,' he said.

'It is not a name,' the man said.

Nikos looked at Renata. He was Greek and not Spanish, and she often wondered whether it was this that made him so non-committal all the time. Of course, he didn't like the name, and here, delivered right into their laps, was a way out of having to succumb to his wife's determination.

Renata said, 'And what is your definition of the word "name"?'

The man remained silent for a moment, his eyes moving between the two of them.

'I would like a precise definition, and a reason that the name we have chosen does not fit with your definition,' Renata said.

The man looked down at the piece of paper still in his hands. Then he got up with great effort and left the room. Renata could not look at her husband, so instead she watched the fan sweeping the room with warm air. She noticed that the rattling sound became more pronounced when the head of the fan was fully turned to either side, but as it reached the middle point of its turning arc, the rattling was almost completely absent. She also noticed that there was a dent in the wire mesh that covered the blades.

'If they will not let us –' Nikos started, but Renata cut him off.

'They will let us,' she said. 'It is not for them to "let" or not. They cannot stop us. They can try to be fascists, but we are not living in a fascist country. It is his name. It is already his name and their paperwork means nothing anyway.'

The baby muttered in her arms. Renata used a corner of the blanket to dab away the line of milk between his lips. She tucked his arm back into the blanket.

'He is hot,' Nikos said.

'He's fine.'

'His face is red.'

'He's fine,' she snapped.

They sat for a moment looking at the desk. Nikos' belly made a noise in the silence. He chuckled and said, 'It's well after lunch.'

'You're thinking about lunch,' Renata said.

He tried to lace his hands on top of his head, but remembered at the last minute that his sunglasses were there. He put his hands back in his lap.

'There should be a computer in here,' he said.

The desk looked oddly empty without a monitor and keyboard. There was a coffee cup on a coaster and a thick file with paper poking out at various angles. There was a pen.

'They must have a database or something,' he said.

Eventually, the man came back in. The room was significantly smaller with him in it, though not because of his size (he was big around the middle, but not anywhere else). He sat down with a heavy grunt, still with the form in his hands, the scruffy hair on top of his head stirring each time the fan's breeze blew through it.

'Well?' Renata said.

'A name,' the man said, 'is a title by which an object or thing is addressed.'

'And where in that definition is there a list of acceptable and not acceptable names?' she said.

'There is no such list.'

'So process the form, please, and then we can go.'

'In our professional judgement,' said the man, 'some names can be deemed detrimental to the child.'

Renata put a hand to her throat. Nikos laid a hand on her upper arm, knowing that she would shrug it off, that it would annoy her further.

'I will speak to your manager now,' she said.

'There are no set parameters,' the man said, 'but we exercise reasonable judgement.'

The window with the broken blind (it sagged on the right-hand side like a deflated accordion) looked out onto the corridor in which they had been sitting before coming into the room. People in suits walked by, peering in occasionally.

'Is there not a family name?' the man asked. 'Your father's name, perhaps. That would make him proud, I'm sure, to have the child named after him.'

'I will not discuss this with you any further,' she said. 'I will speak to your manager.'

The man huffed, looked at Nikos as though the situation were unfair, and he might have the power here to control it, then stood up heavily and left the room again. The baby began to stir. One of his feet came loose from the blankets. When he was born, Nikos had thought he had that disease where the aging process is accelerated, his skin all over was so heavily wrinkled. *Try lying in a bath for nine months,* the midwife had said to him, yet here the boy was weeks later, still the same. An ugly child.

Renata folded the foot back into the blankets and began rocking up and down in the chair. She wasn't looking at Nikos. He could see the thick cords of tension in her neck.

'This doesn't look good,' Nikos said.

She didn't answer him. He hadn't expected her to. He took out his phone and looked at some messages, scrolling through them with his thumb.

The baby carried on shifting, rubbing at his face with both hands. He groaned and sputtered.

'He wants feeding again,' Renata said. 'I can't feed him in here.'

Nikos grunted, looked up at her. 'They have babies in here all the time,' he said.

'I'm not going to feed him in here.'

When the man came back in with another man, Nikos turned the screen off and rested the phone on one of his legs.

The other man was the thinnest man Renata had ever seen. His shoulders were no wider than his waist, which was no wider than his torso. He was a straight line from top to toe, and his clothes hung from him shapelessly. He had a thin moustache traced across his top lip, and his eye sockets cast shadows over his cheeks.

'Hello,' he said, fiddling with a pen as though he'd been disturbed in the middle of writing a report. There was ink on the inside of his thumb.

'Ah,' Renata said dismissively, not quite looking at him.

Nikos shook the man's offered hand by twisting around in the chair.

'This is a small problem we're having, huh?' the thin man said.

'There is no problem at all,' Renata said. 'What problem have you heard about? Nothing is the matter. We are registering his name and then we're gone. So let us do it.'

'Okay,' the thin man said, but it wasn't an okay of agreement. It was the kind of okay that precedes an explanation of why things are not okay. He said, 'We have to discuss, I think, a little about the process here, and about why we have to make certain decisions.'

When Nikos looked at Renata again he saw that she was crying. A tear ran down the line of her jaw. The baby was kicking in her arms and was about to start screaming. She was letting him kick, letting the blanket fall from across his body. His legs and arms were pink with heat, the dark hair plastered across his head. When Nikos stood up, his phone went clattering onto the floor under the desk.

There is more than one kind of home, and more than one way to get there, in Bill Davidson's first Fiction Desk story.

The Short Way Home

Bill Davidson

Patrick Bethany had to walk every day, that was the rule; the one Doctor Monk gave him. It was made easier, and very nearly pleasant, by the close proximity of the park to his house. A pretty park this, and not a big one. The kind where you seldom encountered teenagers, hanging around in that way they do.

Following the cinder path that twisted serpent-like through wide lawns and stands of oak and larch, Patrick could complete the full circuit in about half an hour. Not that this was a half-hour kind of park; just ten years ago he could have gotten round it in fifteen minutes.

He was already puffing those irritating little breaths he'd taken to lately, too fast and shallow to do a person any real good, and his stick was tap, tap, tapping. He'd grown to hate that sound.

Patrick was a tall man who had kept most of his hair, although it was pure white now. He liked to tell the hairdresser, it's gone all thin and faded. Just like me.

What he didn't tell her, because he had never felt comfortable in a brag, was how often his hair had been commented on when he was a young man. Helen used to love to run her fingers through it. Tell him it was like gold.

In the days when he was the golden boy.

Patrick didn't really mind his thinned-out hair, but he hated that damn stick, and he hated his shoes more. Specialist shoes for arthritis, they looked more like especially wide carpet slippers, fuzzy bags with a thick Velcro band to close them. He still had a rack of beautiful shoes and boots at home, handmade some of them because he'd always loved a good shoe, but they would never be worn again, until someone, God knows who, took them to a charity shop.

It was a hazy morning, the sun thinking about burning it off, and there was an agreeable green smell in the air. The birds were in full throat and, though he couldn't see them from where he was, little kids were shouting and laughing nearby, no doubt playing on that fancy new equipment.

Patrick smiled and got into his ungainly walking rhythm, knees picking up his useless feet and planting them flat, so that his toes wouldn't be forced into a bend they could no longer manage.

Just inside the curved archway of the park entrance, he caught sight of something on the path, just in the second that his foot landed on it. He paused and shuffled back. Squinting, he realised it was a baby's bootee, in fine blue wool, a satin ribbon around the ankle. The sort of thing his mother had knitted for every newborn in the Bethany family, for as long as she had been around.

Patrick thought, *this belongs to the family with the laughing kids*. It crossed his mind to pick it up, but bending all that way wasn't an option. Instead, he would wait till he reached the play-park and, if he saw they had a baby, he'd tell them.

But it got him thinking about his mother, if he was honest, for the first time in oh so long. The distance of years between them had grown so great that, even if she crossed his mind, she was inside a re-hash of the same worn out old recollections, so rehearsed they might no longer be real, just the memory of a memory.

But her knitting, that hadn't crossed his mind in decades, which was odd as she had spent so much of her time doing it. The rapid click, click, click of her needles was the soundtrack of his early childhood. People would say, Meg is a fabulous knitter. At a time when most women knitted, she was regarded as a wonder.

She didn't only knit boots and a jacket for the family newborns. She would also knit a ring shawl to bring the baby home in, a shawl so fine that the whole thing could be pulled through a wedding ring. That hardly seemed possible, but she invariably proved it, pulling the material through that tiny space in a kind of ritual performance.

Milly's ring shawl must have been the last one his mother had knitted. Patrick couldn't recall her giving it to him, but he did remember bringing his daughter home in it, her smelling and looking so mind-numbingly *new*. Helen on the passenger seat of the old Austin Cambridge, holding her baby to her chest, looking proud and scared all at the same time.

He'd told her, 'I love you, you know.'

'Of course you do, silly. Don't take on.'

'And I love that baby, even though I've only just met her.'

She laughed, looking at him. 'If you love her now, just you wait.'

As usual, she was as right as a person could naturally be. How he had loved that wild and wilful girl, every scrape she got into feeling like the end of his world.

The bootee on the path was blue, but of course Milly's were pink, his mother being a stickler for that sort of thing. She'd knitted two complete sets of clothes, he recalled now, not knowing if the baby would be a boy or a girl.

It had taken only a few short steps to get from this bootee, to his mother, to Milly, and for the moment he was stalled. A man who had outdistanced everybody, even his own daughter, sometimes he struggled to take another step.

But there was always one to be taken, and soon he got himself into clumsy motion. Coming around the big old oak there was something else in the path, a broken piece of branch or dog turd probably. Not everybody cleaned up.

Getting close, though, it turned out to be a child's sandal. He shook his head, thinking that the family by the swings must be shedding shoes as they went. But he smiled as he reached it, using his stick to turn it over, get a good look.

These sorts of sandals had barely changed over the years. A simple brown leather cap over the toes, perforated in a pattern of diamond shapes, and with a buckle across the ankle. Unlike the bootee, this was a well-worn thing, scuffed and battered. Maybe somebody had dumped it; people did that sort of thing.

The sandal put him in mind not of himself but of Mike, his older brother. He got a sudden, fabulously clear memory of Mike sitting on the wooden bridge over the Frome near their home, swinging his feet in sandals just like those, Patrick copying him because of course he would. The sun sparkled so hard on the water that it hurt.

He made up his mind not to mention the sandal to the family, thinking how it would sound. A bootee and a sandal. What are you, then, the park's shoe monitor?

He was laughing about that when he came across the next shoe. Okay, then this was a deliberate trail, not the first he'd come across in this park by any means. Only a few weeks ago, at Easter, there had been an egg hunt with dozens of kids tearing about, picking up clues and overdosing on chocolate.

A shoe trail. People did such odd things these days.

This next shoe was an older child's, maybe a twelve-year-old, something like that. A plain, black school-type shoe. Patrick wondered if there was a pattern there, baby to toddler to schoolkid. Coming closer, he frowned and bent a little to look.

It was heavily scuffed, this shoe, seriously bashed around and beginning to come apart. And it wasn't quite as plain as it had looked at first sight. It lay sole up, and the bits of rubber not worn away showed the faint imprint of tiny animal tracks.

Patrick barked out a laugh. 'A Pathfinder! You must be nearly as old as me.'

Most of the boys in his class had Pathfinders at one time, it was the thing to have. They came with tiny versions of animal prints on the sole, and a compass in a hidden compartment in the heel. When you stepped in mud, you made miniature versions of rabbit and badger tracks, lions and bears. What was it they said, you were never lost with a Pathfinder?

Patrick stood over the shoe, wondering about the compass, thinking he must have misremembered that. He wanted to pick it up and look at it, find out if there really was one there, but it was such a long way down. He looked around, but nobody was in sight. He shook that away thinking, what was he going to do? Ask somebody to pick the damn shoe up, hand it to him?

Still, he wanted that shoe. He wanted to look in the heel, see if there was really a compass. He leaned his veiny hand heavily on the stick and bent a little, reaching experimentally, but didn't get within a foot of it.

Tutting, he continued his walk, the one the doctor prescribed for him, taking several steps before shuffling back around to the shoe. The Pathfinder.

You're never lost with a Pathfinder.

Patrick thought about it, then manoeuvred the point of his stick into it, but couldn't lift it. He turned his stick around and finally raised it up.

He was painfully aware of how absurd it was to be quite so pleased to have managed this, getting hold of a Pathfinder. A scuffed and ripped up Pathfinder, whose sole was coming away from the upper.

He rubbed his thumb around inside the heel, feeling a droop of disappointment. No compass. He had probably made that up, memories were like that.

Still, he grinned, turning the old shoe over and over. A Pathfinder, after all these years. Peering close, he noticed a tag inside and worried at it with his nail, finally pushing it open to show a compass, looking bright and clean and new. It pointed as cleanly North as ever it did.

'Hah!'

He looked around again, wanting now to share this with someone. *Look, this shoe has a hidden compartment in it. An actual compass, look.* He compressed his lips, knowing perfectly well that his days of sharing anything with anybody were behind him. There was simply nobody to tell.

Something about the shoe brought the memory of a smell, school dinners, whatever they were having it always smelled like cottage pie. Maybe it always *was* cottage pie. He would walk to school with Mike, and ...

No wait, the Bethany boys were never much for walking. The Bethany boys *ran*.

Mike, tall like him, blonde like him and smarter by a mile, was one of the first casualties of the war. One of the ones who didn't come back from Dunkirk.

Well, well. First he'd stumbled onto memories of his mother and her incessant knitting, and now it was himself and Mike, racing each other to school. This wouldn't do. At this rate, he'd be blubbing and people would notice and come across, horror of horrors, to comfort him.

Still, nobody was around. It occurred to Patrick to take the shoe, he wanted it, but that wasn't the right thing to do at all. There was some sort of game going on here. A trail of shoes left, no doubt for children to follow. Odd, but something he ought not to interfere with.

He bent as close to the ground as he could get and dropped it, then continued, wanting to see what was around the bend.

The next shoe was a running spike, and that stalled Patrick for more than a few seconds. It was lying on its side so that he could see the spikes. Another vintage item, from before these things were coloured or fancy, this was leather, the long laces trailing along behind it.

The sharp sound of those spikes on concrete, my God. The smell of sweat, the burn of muscle and the shouts from the crowd. There had been a time, just before the war, when eighteen-year-old Patrick was the third fastest man in Britain, over a hundred yards.

He could barely walk now, but had never entirely forgotten the sensation of flying. Sometimes, just as he fell asleep, he could feel it just a moment away.

At first, he and Mike had trained together, gone to all those little races and meets around the country, but Mike dropped out, his interests taking him different places and all too soon to France.

Patrick had kept going, the ambition to go faster, to be the very fastest, burning harder than the pain in his muscles. That was where he met Helen, the high jumper.

A flash of memory, a recollection he didn't even know he owned, Helen taking a moment on the red clay of the track, tensed like a sprinter. She had been so intense, and so beautiful, that he had held his own breath. Then, all long limbs and determination, she flew at the crossbar, made the height and then turned to grin, hands on hips. No fist pumps or unseemly roaring in those days, but he recalled how desperate he was to get his own hands on those hips. To have that huge smile pointed his way.

Hers were the only hips he ever put his hands to, and that was just fine with Patrick Bethany.

Now he stood above the running shoe, his eyes wet. He never did get to be the fastest, once the war was over, even after his ankle had healed. All those flights over Europe where Patrick navigated through cloud and rain, using techniques they would laugh at now, and the only injury he received was from a piece of shrapnel that sliced open his ankle. He had sat at his shuddering station for almost an hour with a boot full of blood.

Either I lost that spring, or it didn't seem to matter so much anymore.

He sighed and turned his face away, hoping the next shoe would be something modern, one of those coloured trainers that kids wore or something.

It wasn't. It was an RAF pattern flying boot. An almost knee high, heavy calfskin boot, lined with white sheepskin. Only there was nothing white about the inside of this boot: it was bright red, just as it had been when it was pulled off him.

Patrick stood above it, staring at the torn leather at the ankle. He could feel the throb of the engine, the air blowing across his face because the fuselage was shot to hell. The place stunk of smoke and Manny Wallace was dead. Pops. The entire crew but him and Captain Eddie were gone.

Captain Eddie, the bravest man he ever knew, the veteran of over a hundred flights, didn't fly another mission after that night.

No, he didn't want to look at that boot. Didn't want to have a damn thing to do with it. What would be next? The heavy brown brogue of a family man, one who had settled into work in the City and buried first his wife and then his daughter?

It had seemed such a tragedy at the time, but so many people died in car accidents and she was sixty. She still seemed so young, but at least Milly had made it to sixty. Forty years older than Mike.

He was coming to the end of the trail now. Another turn and he'd be back where he started, the entrance to the park, the place where he'd found the little blue bootee. Coming around the bend, there was one last shoe, and it wasn't really so much of a surprise.

A bulky grey slipper shoe, with a Velcro bar strap, double wide so that arthritic fingers could close it. He looked down at his own feet, but he was still wearing both of his. A few steps took him to the slipper shoe, and he bent to pick it up, turning it over and over in his hands.

Both his hands. He blinked and looked around, wondering where he'd misplaced his stick. A few steps further along the path, and a little knot of people came into view at the entrance to the park. They were bending over the figure of a very old man, with white hair that had once been golden, and missing a shoe.

He brought the shoe with him, even though he expected that none of these people would be able to see him. But it seemed that they did, because one by one they turned, smiling, and he realised that he knew them very well indeed.

Kate van der Borgh's latest Fiction Desk story teases apart the threads of home and memory in the lives of its characters. (For more of her work, see 'The History Lesson' in our anthology Separations.*)*

Home, Time

Kate van der Borgh

Betty was watching television when the man walked in. For a minute he stared at her, his face hinting at something like surprise – as if he weren't the one waltzing into her front room unannounced.

'Hello,' Betty said.

The man looked, dumbly. Finally, he murmured: 'Hello.'

Then he walked over to the kitchenette, deposited a carrier bag on the Formica counter and silently unpacked several packets of own-brand custard creams. He paused briefly to adjust the picture that hung above the kettle, the one of the fishermen, the one that didn't belong to her.

Betty shook her head. The problem was, she thought, they didn't pay enough these days. The girls who used to come round, they took the time to chat. Told her about their husbands, their children. Called her Mrs Whitham, all respectful. Foreign, of course, Betty could hardly understand them sometimes, but they always used the right mug. Always left her tray table spotless.

Now, new faces all the time, rushing around. Like this one. Betty watched as the man strode past her armchair to the windowsill and picked up the cut glass vase, causing crisped carnation petals to whisper to the floor.

'Careful of that porcelain dog,' Betty called, trying to sit forward. 'It's very old. I won it, in a sewing competition.'

The man didn't look at her as he made his way to the small sink, holding the vase in outstretched hands like you'd hold a baby with a full nappy.

'That reminds me,' she said to his back, 'I want to make a complaint. They took my sewing machine, but there was nothing wrong with it. It was a Singer, a good one. I'm cross about that. Are you making tea?'

Silently, the man stuffed the wilted blooms into the bin and tipped the vase upside down, noting the sticker on the base declaring it to be *Property of Sycamore Grove Care Home*. Slimy water circled down the plughole. He righted the vase, placed it in the sink and clicked on the little kettle.

Betty didn't suppose the man was all that interested in her sewing machine. That was another shame: she'd talked to the girls about clothes all the time. She loved to tell them about when she was growing up in Nelson, in their terrace with the tin bath and the outdoor toilet, where her mother had been a dab hand with a needle and thread. Her family might not have had two farthings to rub together, but everyone had to admit they'd always been decked out beautifully. Betty could see her mother now, squinting in the lamplight, snapping salvaged thread between her teeth.

In fact, as she'd loved to tell the girls, Betty was wearing a dress from her mother when she first met Richard. All she knew about him – before he made his way across the floor and asked her, in a soft voice that seemed to stop time, for the next dance

– was what her girlfriends had whispered, their voices sweet with Cherry B and lemonade: that he was from a good family, that he worked at his father's law firm. Actually, Betty would have felt a bit inferior, alongside Richard's pristine drape jacket and his gleaming Oxfords, had she not been wearing the dress her mother had altered so finely only a few hours beforehand. Crepe de Chine, in the palest eau de Nil. Yes, she had kept her end up.

Speaking of Richard:

'When is my husband getting here?' Betty asked, fiddling with the cardigan that, like the picture in the kitchen, didn't belong to her.

The man finally spoke, his voice low and lacking warmth. 'Visitors are from ten. So, I guess any minute now.'

*

The man put a cup of tea in front of Betty. He hadn't bothered to ask whether she took sugar, so it was a good job she didn't. But he put out a plate of biscuits, so she decided he must not be totally incompetent. As he leaned over her armchair, adjusting the bib around her neck, she caught the smell of cigarettes on his rumpled sweater.

'That alright for you?' he asked.

'Fine, thank you.'

He retreated to the kitchen area and started to fill the sink with water.

'I used to smoke,' Betty continued, her fingers struggling with the edge of a chocolate digestive. 'But everyone did in the old days. Doctors recommended it, especially – what was it? – menthol. Richard always had his first cigarette at six am sharp while he listened to the radio. The dog sat next to him, sniffing. Ha. It was probably as addicted as him.'

The man dropped some bits and pieces of crockery into the sink, somewhat carelessly, Betty thought, before submerging his hands in the soapy peaks. Solemnly, he began to scrub.

'Nothing should disturb that Condor moment!' Betty announced. 'No, hang on, that was tobacco for pipes. Woodbines! That's what they smoked in the Palace, when I was young. I suppose they still do.'

'You can't smoke in public any more,' the man said, stacking unrinsed bowls onto the wire rack. 'It's been illegal for years.'

'Really?' Betty replied, her voice swooping from low to high in astonishment. 'Well, I didn't know that. I think that's a shame. You could get talking to people over a cigarette.'

And she had, of course. Outside the dance hall, the air still soft with the last of summer. Betty's heart had done the foxtrot when Richard leaned close – always so courteous – to light the cigarette resting on her crimsoned lip, his match momentarily spotlighting their faces like the final frame of a Hollywood film.

That was when he'd asked about her family. And, Lord help her, she'd lied. She'd told him that her father was a manager at Burley's, when in fact he was just one of the many men on the factory floor. Even worse, when Richard drove her home, she'd asked him – oh she feels so awful now – to drop her a couple of streets away, where the front gardens were decorated with driveways and cars rather than lines of greying laundry. She'd had to walk round the side, pretending to go in the back door, before Richard had driven away and given her the chance to scuttle two streets down.

Obviously, when Richard went back the next day to ask Betty to dinner, only to find that the sole resident of 13 Messenger Street was Mister Pilborough the local headteacher, Betty's deception unravelled rather quickly. It was lucky Mister Pilborough knew her real address.

'When did you say my husband was going to be here?'

The man looked at the plastic clock.

'Any minute.'

Afterwards she thought how silly it was that she'd pretended to be from somewhere else. As if Richard wasn't going to find out sometime anyway. But at the time, she was so keenly aware of the differences between her family and his; the truth lay beneath the surface, like the old slip she wore under her delicate green dress. She'd imagined his gleaming Triumph pulling up to number seven, imagined his face falling at the sight of the tiny, concrete garden. His kind expression becoming cold.

No, at the time, she didn't want to lose it – the feeling that seemed to envelop them like music. She wanted the two of them to stay fixed in it forever. No past, no future, just the glorious, enduring moment when his lips finally touched hers.

'Anyway,' Betty said, irritably. 'I want to make a complaint. They took my sewing machine.'

'Right,' the man replied, stifling a sigh.

'It was a good one. A Singer. I'm cross about that.'

*

'Have you far to go?' Betty asked.

'No,' the man replied. 'Only twenty minutes in the car.'

'Oh.' Betty wasn't quite sure what to say. In fact, she wasn't quite sure what they'd been talking about. It happened more and more often: people seemed to move so quickly that they were on to a second thought before she'd got her head around the first. She wished life came with a big remote control, so she could just press pause.

The man turned from the sink and faced her properly for the first time. 'It's a new house, actually,' he continued, as if trying to find something to say. 'I've just moved.'

This chap didn't look like the type to keep much of a home, Betty decided. Like her uncle Barry, whose carpet was matted with dog hair, whose ashtrays were always overflowing. Not like her home with Richard. That was her pride and joy.

When he'd carried her over the threshold that day, she'd giggled like a child. But then, as she'd moved through the rooms, seeing them for the first time, she'd fallen into an awed silence. The sunlight spilling through the bay windows, the feeling of space; the whole house was so bright compared to the dark, cluttered rooms she'd grown up in.

And the kitchen. There, by the window, a shining, stainless steel sink, all sleek and modern. Not like the big pot sink where her father had scrubbed himself after a long day at work. Not forgetting the toilet! No distemper on the walls there. Instead, pink roses climbed gracefully to the ceiling, the wallpaper so crisp she could hardly see the join. Betty was only in the next town, but she felt a million miles from number seven.

The night before, as she'd squeezed the last of her clothes into her new suitcase, her mother had come to her and said: *we'll always be here, love. Home will always be here if you need it.* Betty had laughed, but only to hide the tears that had come unexpectedly to her eyes.

She loved Richard, deeply and surely. And she couldn't wait to share a home with him. She just never realised that your heart could be in two places at the same time.

'Did you leave the broom behind?' Betty asked.

'Pardon?'

'Your broom. You leave it in your old house. It's a sign that you start everything afresh, forget the past.'

'Oh. We never had a broom.'

She was getting tired. 'Where's my husband? When will he be here?'

Of course, Betty went back to number seven a couple of times a week. Sat by the fire, nursing a good, strong cup of tea. One of the last times she was there, long after her father died, Betty had arrived with a roll of sage green crushed velvet under her arm and asked her mother to help her make curtains. She and Richard could have afforded ready-made, obviously. But Betty had told him: sometimes, the old fashioned ways are the best. Better than machine made.

Really, she had just wanted to make something with her mother. She wanted to see that needle and thread moving again, so deftly, between those gentle, expert hands. And perhaps she wanted to step back, just for a moment, into that room where the chimney smoked occasionally, where the laundry hung unashamedly on the rack, where everything had always been and would always be the same.

'He'll be here soon,' the man said, shrugging on his coat. 'See you later, then.'

'Right-ho,' Betty replied. 'Mind how you go.'

The door thumped shut. Couldn't get out the door fast enough, Betty thought.

The curtains, they reminded her – what had they done with her sewing machine? It was a Singer, a good one. But they took it away. She was cross about that.

*

The man practically sprinted down the pavement towards the ageing Punto. After a fumble with the lock, he threw himself into the driver's seat and slammed the door. Behind the windscreen, now dappled with rain, he let the tears run freely down his cheeks.

He'd always known there would be a day when she would no longer recognise him. But when it happened – the unmistakeable absence in her eyes, the realisation that she might never again greet him with her usual 'well hello Jim, lovey'– He wasn't prepared for it, not at all. It had been like looking at a house you used to live in, realising that there were no chairs or tables behind the drawn blinds, no photographs hanging on the walls. The thought dropped into his head, a useless reflex, that he should call her on the phone, like he used to, and tell her: Mum, something really strange happened today . . .

He thumped the steering wheel. He shouldn't have corrected her about smoking in pubs. Not about anything. There was no point. All it did was unsettle her, remind her that the world around her was not quite as she thought it to be. She wouldn't remember the things he told her, anyway. They were gone in a second, birdsong on a breeze.

Even the staff had told him: just go along with it. What did it matter if she thought John Major was still in Downing Street? Or even Harold Wilson? Who cared if she was convinced that Mister Perkins still owned the electrical shop near Bakers' Row?

He'd made that mistake before. The worst was when she'd asked about his father. Mum, he'd said, softly, while she ploughed defiantly on with a plate of microwaved beef stew. Dad died, remember? The confusion, the suffering on her face as the truth had briefly resurfaced – he didn't want to see that ever again.

It was hard to pretend, though. Especially now. When Betty forgot about Richard's death, she brought him back to life. But now it seemed that, to her, Jim had never existed.

He rubbed his eyes roughly with the heels of his hands. At least she'd seemed happy, he told himself. She hadn't smiled at her son, but she'd smiled.

That was something.

A woman passed the car, two small children dragging at her hands. They sang a song, something about a pirate. Going home for tea, he supposed. Just then, a very particular memory came to him, of the house where he grew up: Betty in the sunny kitchen making a shepherd's pie, like she did every Friday, warning him not to pick at the crisped topping before she'd dished up. The plates, with the curly brown pattern on the edges. The scratched, plastic jug – ugly as sin, but it held more gravy than the china one they used 'for best'. He wondered what the children would remember of their own teatime, in later years.

And other things come to him then, moments that seem to belong outside time. Family rituals, like recurring dreams, that will never leave him. Like hearing the ice cream van singing its Greensleeves, that last note always slightly out of tune, and begging his mum for some change (extra raspberry sauce, always, and a Flake). Helping his dad set up the artificial Christmas tree, its silver branches stained yellow from cigarette smoke. All three of them watching the fireworks exploding on the telly, linking arms and singing like they did every New Year.

As the children's voices fade, the man thinks of the invisible distance between him and his mum. As if she's moving through back streets he doesn't know, at the edge of sight, always disappearing around another corner. As if he's calling for her to wait, but she doesn't hear. It's hard. But he'll keep following, as she pulls further and further ahead. He'll listen as she talks about Richard – not even the Richard of his childhood, known for his overambitious DIY jobs, but the one who turned heads as he moved across the floor in a dazzling quickstep. Who knows? Perhaps, another day, the clouds will part just for a second and she'll see him clearly: well hello Jim, lovey.

Jim starts the car, moves away from the kerb. For a few moments he drives in the direction of his old house, his hands on automatic pilot. But he remembers at the last minute, clicks the indicator from left to right. And as he heads towards his new place he imagines Betty smiling as she sits, warm in her armchair, enjoying that cup of tea. Nestled in another home. Sure Richard will be there any minute.

Grief, fish, and twenty-sided dice come together in this nocturnal tale, Gareth Durasow's first Fiction Desk appearance.

The Night Heron

Gareth Durasow

It looked nothing like a heron. It was a squat, shifty-looking bird on chicken stilts, its plume greased back, its pale body braced for all the night had to throw at it; a hunched silhouette of the utmost patience, primed to stab the water with its face knife.

'*Nycticorax nycticorax*,' said Dad. 'Your mum taught me that. They're very rare in this country. I think that one's male, but I wouldn't put money on it.'

I tried the word myself: *Nyct-i-cor-ax, nyct-i-cor-ax.*

It sounded like the start of a witch's spell, the kind that might bring Mum back, but not in a way I'd like.

I tried racing Dad to the bottom of the can. His was the kind that he could only ever drink two of; mine was the kind that made me burp sweet fizz out of my nose when I drank too fast.

'Right,' he said. 'Reckon we've got enough slugs.'

The gloss-black beasts slimed their way up the inside of our umbrella. It sounded like they were unzipping the fabric with their bellies. Dad unplugged every single one and chucked them in a bait box.

I'd got a bet on with Hector – which one of us could land the biggest fish – and Dad said he'd help me. He'd said it would be a late one. I'd have to stay up well past my bedtime and if I complained about being bored I'd be for the high jump.

We loaded the boat up with the rods and the tackle. No doubt it seemed a lot of faff to the night heron, which had paused mid-stride, like he was playing grandmother's footsteps with something only he could see. I imagined that when the time came for him to break his silence, he'd croak his own name: 'Nycticorax! Nycticorax!'

A whole classroom's worth of obsolete equipment jutted up from the shallows. Dad used an oar to poke us around the corners of desktop monitors and computers, their hard drives loaded with schoolwork that was probably older than me.

The boat skulked along, and I imagined we were a pair of hooded rogues up to no good – that the blinking blips on Dad's app weren't lurking fish, but monsters waiting to strike. The only way we could've looked more the part was if our fishing rods had been the kind of blades that can take a life with a sound no louder than someone whispering a name.

There was a squall of feedback from Dad's phone. 'This is our spot,' he said, and the boat slowed as if he'd told it to.

He cast out for me. After last time, he didn't trust me not to put the hook in his ear. The line sizzled away from us and sank with a slug-heavy *sploosh!*

'We won't have to wait long,' he said, and by God he meant it: the rod veered off immediately, like a dowsing stick finding water.

'Are you going to reel it in or what?'

I cranked the reel, round and round, and all the time I felt the heat of Dad's stare on the side of my face. It was that same feeling as when you rub your hands together, as fast as you can, and then hold your palms half an inch from each other. Finally, the skinny fish flailed in the air and came careening like a bungie jump gone wrong to land in Dad's glove.

Me, one. Nycticorax, nil.

Dad rooted around inside the fish's head to free the hook.

'Will that do you?' he asked.

He watched me pretend to look satisfied and laughed, and then couldn't laugh for coughing.

'I'm having you on – you'll not win anything with this tiddler. It's just the bait. Pass me the chopping knife. It's in that box.'

The parts he didn't need went into the reeds.

'There's a potato peeler in there. Take the scales off while I change the line.'

I set about shredding fish scales into the water.

Meanwhile, the night heron had come to life. His head twisted this way and that, like he was trying to wind up a pocket watch with the end of his beak. Whatever he'd caught, it had legs and wasn't going down the hatch easily. He chugged it like Dad chugged his lager.

One all.

'Dad, what do night herons eat?'

'Fish, frogs, mice. Anything that'll fit down their neck, I guess. Get close enough and he'd probably have your tongue out, or your eyeball.'

He saw my face.

'I'm kidding, spud.'

He swapped the hook for a bigger one, one that looked about the right size for catching a pit bull terrier. I imagined the dog locked on the line, thrashing its terrible meathead from side to side, paws planted on the boat as it tried to lever itself back into the murk.

Dad asked, 'Have you done yet?'

I handed him the badly shaved chunk – 'That'll do,' he said – and he crammed it onto the hook.

The line went out again and he told me to throw some bait along with it too, for good measure. Most of the maggots in the box had turned to casters so I didn't mind putting my hand in so much; I could just pretend they were Rice Krispies. I flung them so hard my shoulder hurt for a whole week after, but even so, they fell short of the landing spot.

Dad gave me the look: *I could say something, but I won't.*

Instead, he opened another can and made himself comfortable in the bows.

'You might as well get comfy, because this'll take a while.'

It was like he was some kind of freshwater clairvoyant, a fish whisperer. If he said it'd be a quick bite, it'd be quick; if he said we were in for a wait, get out the playing cards.

I took a die from my pocket and dropped it onto the bait box lid. If I could roll a twenty then that meant we'd land the biggest fish you've ever seen. I re-rolled, again and again, and it was only when the die fell into the bottom of the boat for the second time that Dad told me to pack it in.

'Your mum and I used to come here on a weekend – we can't have been much older than you. She would've swum out here all day if your gran would've let her. I couldn't swim to save my life back then. I used to just float on my back, enjoying the sun.'

He sifted through the bait box like he was looking for popcorn. For a moment I thought he was going to absent-mindedly swallow the caster he'd picked up.

'Then, someone at school told me that a farmer lost one of his cows in here, and that put paid to me swimming. I couldn't bear the thought of it rotting underneath us while your mum and I swam about, getting the water in our mouths, splashing each other with it. So from that day on, I used to watch her from the bank – just over there, more or less where that heron's stood. I never told her the real reason why I stopped swimming here – what you don't know doesn't hurt you, I suppose. I just didn't want to spoil the water for her. Looking back, I was an idiot. There'll be that much dead stuff in here that the odd cow probably wouldn't make a blind bit of difference in the grand scheme of things.'

He squeezed the chosen caster between thumb and forefinger until it popped and turned to juice.

Dad's phone rang, the same awful ringtone as those old phones where you had to put your finger in the hole and spin it round.

'Who on earth's ringing me at this time?'

He picked his phone up and looked at the screen for a while.

Unknown caller, it said.

I asked, 'Aren't you going to answer it?'

'No, I'm spending time with my heir.'

He placed it on the side of the boat and watched it ring. Then, when it didn't stop, he nudged it overboard. I leaned over the side and watched its low-bellied light fall away. There was no chance I was putting my hand in after it.

I asked: 'Why did you do that?'

'Because every time it rings, I think it's your mum: Where have you go to? Dinner's on; how long are you going to be? And then, when it isn't her, it makes me want to do something like . . . well, like that.'

We listened to the lake. It had little to say. All it could do was copy us whenever we spoke loudly enough. I imagined I could still hear Dad's phone. I wondered if it had reached the bottom yet, or was still on its way down, so many curious little fish lit up by the screen light. Then it occurred to me: 'Couldn't you have just changed your ringtone?'

'Don't know how,' he said. 'Besides, it wouldn't have felt anywhere near as good.'

He chuckled to himself.

I asked him: 'Weren't you using it to find the fish?'

He said the F-word. F for forbidden.

Over his shoulder, I saw the night heron lance something in the grass.

'Look at that,' I said, and Dad followed my finger.

'Looks like a mouse, or maybe it's a vole. Whatever it is, it's a goner.'

Again, the winding of the pocket watch.

Nycticorax, two.

Me, one.

'She would've loved to see that fella again. She'd have probably gone over there and hand-fed him. My little twitcher.'

The rod flexed, so hard and so quickly I wasn't sure how it didn't snap in half.

'Dad, I think you got something.'

'No, you have.'

Which was his way of saying get on with it then.

In the end, he had to take over, so I didn't end up in the drink with his favourite rod. I watched the battle unfold: Dad nearly over the side, giving a little slack when required, spooling in a little when the time was right. Whatever it was, it had to be wrestled into the boat with all our hands. Dad swore so vividly you'd have thought it was a baby alligator, and when I matched him swear for swear, he didn't clip me like all the times before.

He had his knees either side of it to keep it from retreating over the side. It had little stubby whiskers and gills wide enough to slip your hand in up to the knuckles, deep enough for Dad's wedding ring to vanish inside when he hoisted it up.

'Is this one big enough for you?'

I thought of Hector showing me his phone next weekend, Hector having to hold his fish from the top of a step ladder so it had enough height for the mouth to just touch the ground: 'That's nothing. Look what I caught!' Hector with his bet-winning monster, long as a phone box, heavy as Hector.

'Stick or twist,' said Dad. 'What are we doing?'

'Can we use this one for bait, like we did the other?'

'You want to use this fish to catch an even bigger fish?'

He'd said it with just the right amount of impossible; Dads are good at that.

I asked, 'Do you think there is a bigger fish out here?'

'I know there's a bigger fish.'

'Then I want to catch it.'

'And you won't wimp out when you have to hold it?'

The thought of it, aground in the mud, longer than the boat and stinking of lakebed; its mouth a raised portcullis, big enough to walk into . . .

'I won't wimp out.'

'Good lad.'

I looked to the night heron, and it didn't bat an eyelid.

We end this anthology as we began it, bidding farewell to another family home, in this story from Fiction Desk newcomer Clarissa Dennison.

Pots

Clarissa Dennison

'Oh Mrs Tregear, how superb, a full-length S-Plan!' says the man from Bonham's, walking into the living room. Young and thin in his close-fitting suit – full beard, no tie – as vain as they come, probably. 'And the curtain fabric, original Lucienne Day Calyx, yes?'

'You recognise them? I'm so glad.' In her thick cardigan, her eighty-year-old arthritic hip throbbing, Margaret gleams with delight. 'My husband and I married in 1951 and the Festival of Britain was on; we loved the new ideas.'

'The whole room is lovely. It's an awful shame to dismantle it, really.'

Margaret knows it is lovely. The long line of steel-framed windows that turn a corner, bringing the green of the garden in, the fitted window seats, the teak furniture that dances on delicate pointed legs, and of course, the Calyx curtains, which also have delicate, balancing things on them (flowers or goblets) teetering on slender stems and dissolving into abstract shapes that shoot across the background in strong diagonals. She never tires of the colour scheme: a muted mustard-yellow and grey, with dabs of black and white and tiny touches of scarlet. She made herself a Calyx dress too, for France that summer: full skirted, tight waisted, scoop necked; it was quite . . . but the young man is speaking again.

'The sideboard alone will fetch around two thousand. We'll save your things for our special 'Mid-Century Modern' sale in April, to attract the specialist collectors.'

'But they're not modern now, are they? My daughter calls them fuddy-duddy.'

'Ah, but Modern doesn't mean new anymore. We use the word Contemporary for that. Modern is a period, what the common man calls Retro. The younger generation are warming to it, but your daughter not?'

'She's a social worker, very practical.'

Margaret is confused: so Modern is old now; she too is old, and Norman, who was always modern, is now so old that he's dead. Everything must be sold, and she must move to Essex. She offers the Bonham's man a cup of tea, realising too late what that entails. Dragging her bad hip to the kitchen she tentatively lifts the kettle. On a bad day, her fingers could suddenly crumple with pain, loosening their hold. It has already happened once or twice and she has scars to show for it, which is one of the reasons she is moving closer to Laura. Not in with Laura, just closer; in a flat down the road. Laura is very insistent. Today the fingers hold out, nonetheless.

'I'll send someone to look at those books. There could be some value there . . . first editions.'

The once-glossy books of cave paintings with their colour illustrations – rare back then – now have faded dust-jackets hanging in brittle shreds: *Lascaux*, *Altamira*, *Niaux*: the titles are evocative, particularly Niaux, where she worked over several summers with Norman. The superb Palaeolithic paintings that she came to know so intensely in the shadowy caves; red wine on the tongue under the umbrella pines as the cicadas thrummed; Norman's tanned forearms holding a clipboard.

The Bonham's man slurps his tea. How long has she been ignoring him? But he smiles warmly. She hardly knows if she is elated or lifted on a great wave of sadness. Life came to an end a month ago when Norman died, yet today she has been living.

'It must be hard saying goodbye to all this. I hope you're able to take a few things with you?'

'A few, yes, thank you.'

He stands to go. For Margaret, it is now or never.

'Before you go, could you possibly help me for a few minutes?' He looks hesitant, frightened almost, but no matter. 'It's just that I want to go upstairs. I live downstairs now, but there's something I'd like to have a last look at.'

'I could bring it down for you?'

'No, you couldn't. You'll understand when you see. I can manage the stairs if you come behind, just in case I trip.'

'Yes, yes of course.'

She begins the slow climb, grunting. He matches her pace with little child steps, two feet on each stair, awkwardly chatting, and there are no mishaps. On the landing she picks up a torch and opens the door to a small dark bedroom. The flickering beam reveals that the room is empty. But the walls themselves are full: shaggy, reddish-brown forms, faces, horns, massive flanks and delicate legs. A herd of wild horses dances towards them with manes erect; from behind emerge two huge white bulls, confronting each other with lowered horns; in the distance a herd of deer graze. On the ceiling are more animals, and from the darker corners other forms creep, human possibly. Margaret's gaze lingers; she turns in a slow circle, arms outstretched. He is no longer making polite conversation but is visibly overwhelmed.

'Oh my God ... is it Lascaux?' She nods. 'You did this yourself? You're an artist.'

'Just a copyist. It was my job you see, recording what we found.'

'It's staggering ... and you have to leave it.'

'I'll take my paints.'

She is on the landing now, putting a foot on the first downward step.

'Wait,' he says sharply. 'I'd better go first.'

He squeezes carefully past. She manages a few stairs, then a leg buckles, a foot turns. He leans clumsily into her. Suddenly she is spread-eagled on her front, her open mouth tasting the stair carpet, but he has hold of her. They slide slowly downward together; she feels his slight weight, smells his cologne. At the bottom she realises, heart pounding, that they are all right: just a few buttons off her cardigan, the Calvin Klein suit a bit rumpled.

He speaks first: 'I'd better get some help.'

'Don't be silly. I'm perfectly fine.'

'Well, let me make you some tea, at least.'

It is while they are having tea that the telephone rings. It is Laura.

'Mum? A bit of bad news I'm afraid. Don't worry, nobody's died. It's just ... the flat's fallen through.'

'I see.'

'It'll be hard to find another ... there's only a week ... come to us ... better really ... a bit risky on your own.'

The words reach Margaret in snatches; her concentration comes and goes.

'To you?'

'Yes, it's fine, you can have the back sitting room . . . shower and loo . . . everything you need.'

The Bonham's man is looking at a book, out of politeness, successfully avoiding listening.

Margaret sees him stand and come towards her, but it is only to say goodbye.

'I have another appointment. If you're sure there are no bones broken, no need for the ambulance?'

'Oh, no, really. Look!' She turns in a cumbersome pirouette, which takes effort, but she really doesn't want the ambulance. If they could just stay drinking tea . . .

'It's been a real pleasure meeting you, and seeing your lovely things. I know time's short, so I'll get the book man to drop in tomorrow. Then we can collect on Friday. Will that be okay?'

'Oh, yes.'

'Goodbye Mrs Tregear, and all the best with your move.'

Margaret subsides onto the sofa and stares at the Calyx curtains, which will have to come with her, into Laura's back room.

*

It smells like boiling fish, thinks Laura, waking at six-thirty on a busy work morning. She stumbles downstairs through a stinking miasma to the kitchen where her mother stands in a dressing-gown, chopping shallots. A saucepan-lid rattles over a head of steam; lifting it, Laura sees a circle of glassy eyes.

'Honestly Mum, fish heads! First thing in the morning!'

'It's bouillabaisse.'

'But I want tea.'

'Silly, it's not for now. It has to simmer all day, to develop the flavour.'

Laura's husband, Joe, comes into the kitchen.

'What's cooking?'

'Bouillabaisse.'

'French fish soup? You made that once before, it was delicious.'

'It has to be done right. It's no good if it doesn't have all day to cook.'

'I suppose you saw it done right when you worked in France. Real slow food. Wasn't that where you met Norman?'

'Indeed, it was. You remember that.' She likes Joe, he takes more time. It must be the cabinet-making, the slow attention to detail.

'But not here, not now!' says Laura. 'It's making me sick. I have to be in court in an hour. I can't be smelling of fish.' She lifts the pan and carries it out to the back doorstep.

Feeling tears coming, Margaret retreats to her room. On the table are paints, a small tube of superglue, a plain white vase, and a book of cave paintings open at a page where a bison appears to hover in mid-air, massive, shaggy, with delicately drawn face and hooves. If she can get it right, the animal will float majestically over the belly of the vase. It's a poor substitute for painting on the wall, but she is not completely crazy; she'd never get away with that here. In the month she has been here, she has painted almost every day, so there are already nearly thirty painted pots arranged over the furniture. Joe's hand-made solid ash and beech set them off excellently. And he likes her pots: each lunchtime she shows him what she has done. They talk too, about the stone-age hunter-gatherers who painted the originals, wondering what compelled them to work away in semi-darkness by the light of little stone oil lamps to express so exactly the spirit of the animals they hunted. What compels her to copy them? She doesn't discuss that with Joe.

After lunch she allows herself ten minutes on her laptop. She finds a holiday cottage in the foothills of the Pyrenees and makes a July booking, choosing the higher rate which permits free last-minute cancellation. Then she checks her long list of other bookings. It's a game, of course: not being completely crazy yet, she will cancel them in good time. Her taxi arrives. She is going to town to buy paint, because Laura cannot be trusted to tell the difference between 'burnt sienna' and 'umber'. The taxi will drop her at the centre and she will hobble around for an hour or so and go for coffee.

All goes smoothly until, coming out of the covered shopping mall, the wind hits her and a sheet of rain descends. She pushes through it and sees a long queue of raincoated figures in the coffee shop. Exhaustion and pain descend suddenly. She must sit down. Next moment she is sitting on the kerb, legs stretched awkwardly into the teeming gutter. A concerned crowd surrounds her.

'A taxi ... yes please ... I have plenty of money.'

But there are no taxis to be seen. She is helped up, guided into the café and bought hot tea; someone stands to give her a seat. So much fuss: hateful and embarrassing. She finally remembers her phone, and phones the house. Joe will come for her, but he sounds subdued, and driving home he is unnervingly silent. When they arrive, Laura stands silhouetted in the doorway. Margaret sees her screaming face, but can hear nothing through the storm until she is inside.

'How could you, Mum? You're crazy, degenerate ... no, I mean demented, gone in the head! So cruel to Joe. Oh, come in, quick and close the door.'

In the hall, Margaret stands in sick blackness for a moment and drops to the floor.

'Oh God, call an ambulance, she's had a stroke. No, she's coming round ... Mum, Mum, are you okay?'

'Let go of me, I don't want your help.'

She can remember every word her daughter has said. She heaves herself onto hands and knees but is then stuck. Joe, without a word, takes hold of her under the armpits, helps her crawl to the sofa, and brings her a glass of water. Laura begins again:

'We know your little secret now, you see. The roof leaked so we went into your room; there was water pouring through a hole in your ceiling. I wanted to move everything, lift the carpet, save some of Joe's furniture, but it was much too late for that, wasn't it? All that beautiful furniture that's taken him hours and hours, dovetailing, planing, waxing... you've gone and glued your bloody vases to it!'

Margaret cannot speak. She must somehow get to her room. Joe helps her, silently. It is in disarray: water dripping from a hole in the ceiling into a bucket, everything shoved aside, books in piles, paint spilled. Her pots are still in their places, of course. A small lid must have broken as Laura tried to wrench a teapot from the table, but that is all.

'Margaret, let's sit down and talk.'

Joe in the doorway, his first words to her since lunchtime. She offers him a chair.

'Laura's right, I do love making this stuff. All that daytime work fitting kitchens, that's just to put food on the table. But this...' He runs his hand over the smooth grain of a piece of ash, turns it almost caressingly over the corner. 'I don't want them to be museum pieces, I want them used. But what you've done ... I just don't get it.'

'Stop Joe,' says Margaret 'Please, let me say sorry. I know I shouldn't have done it. But these pots I paint . . . well, in a way they mean to me what your furniture means to you. they're part of me and what I'm good at. Part of my past... and Norman.'

'Yes, and I think they're lovely, but why glue them down?'

'That's the thing, I have to. I wouldn't paint them if I couldn't stick them. It would be too risky.'

'What?'

'I couldn't rely on them being there. They could go . . . or be taken.'

'I don't understand, there's a burglar alarm, and you know we would never – '

'Of course, I know that. It's not logical. I'm a mad old woman. But after all that's happened – Norman going, selling the house, coming here – I just need something to be reliable, permanent.'

'I think I see what it means to you Margaret, but even so, you've ruined my stuff. I thought you were more . . .'

Joe's mouth quivers, then he sobs. Laura comes and stands behind him, her hands on his shoulders. She tells her mother she will never forgive her.

So, this is what it's like, getting old: losing touch, losing sense, making a mess. Resenting and being resented. Impossible really.

'Could you leave me alone for a bit, please?'

When they have gone, Margaret pulls a book from her shopping bag, chosen carefully for Laura by accessing her online 'wishlist' and bought in town this afternoon: *Tackling Social Injustice*. Just up Laura's street. She will never get it now. Margaret stuffs it under the bed, opens her laptop and brings up her holiday bookings. The cottage in Niaux is available all year round and she books it for six months, which costs most of what she has in the bank, even at the 'non-refundable' rate. She will get there somehow.

The man from Bonhams might have understood. But probably not.

About the Contributors

Zeph Auerbach is a teacher and writer from London. His short plays have been performed at the Edinburgh Fringe and the Science Fiction Theatre Festival. He once tweeted the entire life of Ludwig Wittgenstein over six months, and liked doing it so much that he did the same for Philip K Dick and Kurt Vonnegut. He enjoys swimming, gaming, and writing stories that involve the breaking of some fundamental aspect of reality. More of Zeph's writing can be found at zephauerbach.com

Kate van der Borgh grew up in Burnley, Lancashire, and left her home town to study music at Cambridge. She then moved to London, where she packed up her bassoon and became a business writer.

As well as writing fiction in her spare time, she enjoys opera, trash telly, ghost stories, and worrying about everything.

Alastair Chisholm writes short stories and children's books. His picture book *The Prince and the Witch and the Thief and the Bears* was shortlisted for the Scottish Book Trust Bookbug Prize, and his debut children's science fiction novel *Orion Lost* was nominated for the Carnegie Medal. You can find him on Twitter at @alastair_ch, or on his website at www.alastairc.com.

Alastair lives in Edinburgh with his wife, two children, and a cat, and he thinks it's weird to refer to himself in the third person. He likes biscuits.

Andrew Cochrane is a writer based in Southampton, where he lives with his wife and two daughters. He holds a master's degree in creative writing, and has previous work placed at *Litro*, *Every Day Fiction*, *Words for the Wild*, and *Postcard Shorts*. He is currently seeking representation for his debut novel, which explores the effects of the Grenfell Tower fire on the residents of a tower block on the south coast.

Bill Davidson is a Scottish writer of mainly speculative fiction. His debut novel *The Orangerie* will be released in 2021 by Close to the Bone Publishing and his first collection of short stories *New Gods, Old Monsters* was released in 2020 by Dark Lane Books. In the past four years he has placed well over fifty short stories with publications around the world including Ellen Datlow's *Best Horror of the Year* anthology. Find him on billdavidsonwriting.com or @bill_davidson57.

Clarissa Dennison was born and raised in Norwich, and spent some years in Cambridge and London before moving to Northern Ireland in 1986. She worked as a counsellor until retiring in 2014. She loves walking on the North Antrim coast and in the wood which she planted twenty-five years ago on the family farm near Antrim. Occasionally she will muster the energy for small adventures, but usually prefers to stay at home, cooking, reading, and writing. She is married with two grown-up sons.

Jacki Donnellan has lived in the Netherlands since moving there from Hampshire in 2002. She has been a lawyer and a stay-at-home mum and is now a qualified English language teacher as well as a writer of flash and short fiction. Her stories have been published both in print and online. You can find her on Twitter: @Donnellanjacki and on Facebook: Jacki Donnellan-writer

Gareth Durasow grew up in Castleford. His short stories and poetry have been published by *Dead Ink*, *Neon*, *The Rialto*, *Ellipsis*, *Shearsman*, *The Molotov Cocktail*, and *Ad Hoc Fiction*. He is a *STORGY* flash fiction prize winner. His poetry collection *Endless Running Games* is available from Dog Horn Publishing. He holds an MA in Theatre Studies from the University of Leeds.

Toby Wallis lives in Suffolk. His writing has won *Glimmer Train*'s Short Story Award for New Writers, and been shortlisted for The Bridport Prize, The Raymond Carver Short Story Contest, and the Brick Lane Bookshop Short Story Prize. He has a website at tobywallis.net and is on twitter as @tobyshmoby.

For more information on the contributors
to this volume, please visit our website:

www.thefictiondesk.com/authors

Also Available

the first thirteen Fiction Desk anthologies:

1. Various Authors
2. All These Little Worlds
3. The Maginot Line
4. Crying Just Like Anybody
5. Because of What Happened
6. New Ghost Stories
7. There Was Once a Place
8. New Ghost Stories II
9. Long Grey Beard and Glittering Eye
10. Separations
11. New Ghost Stories III
12. And Nothing Remains
13. Somewhere This Way